"*Horse* is a deeply moving narrative that captures the essence of healing and transformation. Through the entwined lives of Jason Masters, a combat veteran, and a wild mustang, it explores themes of trust, survival, and the power of connections. This novel is not only a testament to the resilience of the human spirit but also a profound commentary on the silent bonds that can heal us. A captivating and emotionally charged journey, it's a must-read for anyone who believes in the possibility of second chances and the healing power of nature."

***

This book "Horse" hit me hard. I'm an old Vietnam vet. Been through hell and back. Dr. Ferruolo's horse thing saved my life. No joke.

I was messed up bad. Nightmares. Angry all the time. Couldn't talk to nobody. Then I went to this horse place. Didn't think it would do shit. But it did.

This book? It's like being back there. The guy Jason, he's just like me. Hurting. Lost. Then he meets this horse. It all came back to me. How I felt when I first touched that big animal. How it didn't judge me. Just was there.

Dr. Ferruolo gets it. He writes it real. No fancy stuff. Just the truth. How it feels to be broken. How them horses help you put the pieces back together.

Reading this book, I remembered stuff I learned at the farm. Good stuff. Stuff that helps me get through bad days. It ain't always easy, but it's better.

This ain't no make-believe story. It's real as dirt. If you're hurting like I was, read this book. It might just save you too. And if you ain't a vet, read it anyway. Maybe you'll understand us better.

Dr. Ferruolo, he's one of us. He knows. This book, it's like he reached in my head and wrote down what's in there. It ain't pretty, but it's true.

This book, it's important. Real important. Read it. That's all I gotta say.

***

"Horse" is an absolutely captivating read! Dr. Ferruolo's writing pulled me in from the first page, and I found myself deeply invested in Jason's journey. The way the author weaves together themes of trauma, healing, and the bond between humans and animals is masterful. I've never been around horses much, but this book gave me a new appreciation for these majestic creatures and their potential to help heal wounded souls. A must-read for anyone interested in stories of personal growth.

***

As a fellow veteran, I found "Horse" to be an emotionally challenging but ultimately rewarding read. The portrayal of PTSD and moral injury is spot-on. I saw a lot of my own struggles reflected in Jason's character. The book definitely doesn't shy away from the harshness of combat trauma, but it also offers hope through Jason's healing journey. While some parts were tough to get through, I appreciate the honesty and the message that recovery is possible. Highly recommend for vets and their families.

***

As someone who works in equine-assisted therapy, I was blown away by the accuracy and depth of "Horse." Dr. Ferruolo clearly knows his stuff when it comes to natural horsemanship and the therapeutic potential of human-horse interactions. The way he describes the subtle communication between Jason and the Mustang is beautifully done and aligns perfectly with what we see in our work. This book is a great story and an excellent resource for explaining the benefits of equine therapy to clients or skeptics. I'll be recommending it to colleagues and clients alike.

***

Dr. Dave Ferruolo's "Horse" is a powerful exploration of trauma recovery and the therapeutic potential of human-animal bonds. As a mental health professional, I was impressed by the in-depth portrayal of PTSD and moral injury. The author doesn't offer easy solutions but instead shows the complex, often non-linear nature of healing. The integration of equine-assisted therapy concepts is well-done and provides food for thought about alternative treatment modalities. It's a thoughtful and engaging read that I would recommend to both colleagues and patients interested in exploring different approaches to trauma recovery.

About Dr. Dave Ferruolo

Dr. Dave Ferruolo's latest book, *HORSE*, presents an inspiring fusion of his life's work and passion. With a background as a Navy SEAL and a distinguished career in the mental health industry as a psychotherapy, Dr. Dave brings a wealth of experience to his writing. His expertise in natural horsemanship and equine-assisted psychotherapy adds a unique depth and compassion to the narrative, making it not just a book but a journey toward understanding resilience and healing.

His transition from military service to mental health advocacy is reflected in the authenticity and insightfulness of his storytelling. Holding a doctorate that explores the healing benefits of working with horses for veterans, Dr. Dave embodies the spirit of innovation in therapeutic practices. He's a storyteller and a beacon of hope, offering a fresh perspective on overcoming adversity through the bonds between humans and horses.

HORSE is more than a story; it's an exploration of the soul, a testament to the healing power of connection, and a call to action for those seeking empowerment and healing. Dr. Dave's narrative invites readers to engage with their own stories of resilience, guided by the profound relationships that can develop between humans and animals.

drdavebooks.com

HORSE

HORSE

DR. DAVE FERRUOLO

Dr. Dave Books

Dr. Dave books
Laconia, NH 03247
drdavebooks.com

ISBN 978-1-963834-00-0
ISBN 978-1-963834-01-7

Printed in the United States of America
10 9 8 7 6 5 4 3 2 1 0

Cover Design by Dr. Dave Ferruolo

First Printing, 2024

Paul C. Smith
1960-2016

Paul was not just a mentor; he was a friend. Our paths intertwined through our love for horses, a shared thirst for knowledge, and an unquenchable zest for adventure. Our ideas resonated; our philosophies aligned, and our visions were mirrored. Paul's guidance transformed me into a better horseman and, more importantly, a better human being. His wisdom was instrumental in shaping my approach to horses. He played a pivotal role in the development and success of my equine veteran programs. Paul was an invaluable supporter of my doctoral research on the impact of equine-assisted therapies for combat veterans.

Our journey was filled with ideas and plans for the future. A vivid memory that stands out is a conversation with Paul after reading his dissertation, *Path of the Centaur*. I suggested he turn it into a book; but Paul, ever the pragmatist, preferred action over words. He believed in the power of doing rather than documenting.

Recently, I revisited *Path of the Centaur* and

felt a deep conviction that its essence needed to be shared. This novel is a tribute to Paul Smith and his contributions to the equine-assisted learning and therapy world. The knowledge encapsulated in *Path of the Centaur* breathes life into the chapters of this book. In a symbolic gesture, the protagonist's father embodies the essence of Paul's sagacity, continuing his legacy of insight and inspiration.

Supporting Veterans and Horses

A portion of the proceeds from this book will go to supporting veteran equine-assisted therapy and learning programs and non-profits focused on rescuing and rehabilitating maltreated horses for this work.

CONTENTS

HORSE emerges as a narrative steeped in the dual essence of resilience and renewal. It's a tale where my fervor for creativity, adventure, and the untamed beauty of Colorado's landscapes melds with a deep reverence for horses. This story also sheds light on a poignant reality—the struggles faced by our nation's veterans as they navigate the turbulent journey back to civilian life. From battling PTSD and societal reintegration to overcoming the stigma of mental health issues, the parallels between their experiences and those of rescue horses are strikingly similar. Both have faced their own battles—veterans with their wars and horses with neglect and abuse—each seeking solace and a sense of belonging in a world that often feels alien.

My journey into rescuing horses and embracing

natural horsemanship principles not only offered these majestic creatures a second chance but also paved my path toward healing. It inspired a profound realization: the therapeutic synergy between veterans and rescue horses. This revelation became the cornerstone of my mission to weave together my passion for equine welfare with my commitment to supporting veterans' mental health. The creation of equine-assisted programs for veterans, utilizing rescue horses, is more than a testament to my personal evolution—it's a tribute to the transformative power of compassion, understanding, and the unspoken language of healing that transcends species. *HORSE* is not just a story; it's a journey of discovery, healing, and the magic that happens when two worlds, seemingly disparate, find common ground and mutual redemption.

~ Dr. Dave Ferruolo

CHAPTER 1

The Ascent to Failure

Jason Masters' fingers clenched tightly around the jagged edge of the cliff. Below him, the world was a blur—a mosaic of greens and browns that swirled dizzily in the depths. His breath was ragged, matching the erratic rhythm of his heart that thundered in his chest. With its unforgiving steepness and treacherous terrain, the cliff was his chosen challenge, a relentless pursuit of conquering nature and his inner demons.

This climb was not average—not even less traveled. It was a route no one had braved before. It was not considered a viable climb. The attributes of this cliff were too brutal, too impassable for serious contemplation. Jason had conquered many of Colorado's *Holy Grails:* Longs Peak, Mount Wilson, El Diente, Little Bear, and Capitol Peak, among others. These peaks were formidable. Yet, this challenge was something altogether different. It was a goliath unknown. A silent giant looming in the background of Jason's life. A lure that he had been surveying since childhood. This was a personal apex, a monolith that had beckoned through the years, whispering a challenge he could no longer ignore.

The sun beat down mercilessly, searing his exposed skin as beads of sweat mingled with the dust on his brow. He could feel every muscle in his body straining against gravity; each fiber stretched to its limit. The air was thin here, each breath a battle against the altitude that sought to claim him as its own.

Jason's ascent was a relentless battle against the mountain, his body being pushed to its limits. Then, in a heart-stopping moment, his foot slipped. The gritty sound of his rubber-soled shoe scraping against the rock was the only warning before he slid, his side harshly scraping against the jagged surface. Panic surged through his veins as he scrambled desperately for a hold. His skin tore against the unforgiving wall, leaving a trail of flesh and blood in its wake. Every nerve in his body screamed in alarm, a primal instinct for survival kicking in.

Jason jammed his fingers into a narrow crevice in a desperate bid to arrest his descent. The sudden stop was jarring, wrenching his shoulder, sending a searing pain through his arm. His fingers bent at an unnatural angle, a sharp agony indicating a sprain or worse. He hung there for a moment, gasping for breath, his heart pounding in his ears. His eyes locked in the distance. He could almost make out his parent's farm amongst the distant expanse of the San Luis Plains. The world seemed to spin around him, a dizzying array of sky and stone that blurred into one. He knew this was a precarious situation, the edge between continuing his climb and a fall that could mean his end. This slip was a brutal reminder of the mountain's power and his vulnerability in the face of its towering might.

As Jason re-initiated his ascent, the world below seemed to recede into a distant memory, leaving only the sky's vast expanse above and the uncompromising rock before him. Each movement now bore the weight of his determination and the fresh sting of his wounds. The scratches and bruises along his side burned with every motion. His sprained fingers throbbed painfully, compromising his grip; his twisted shoulder sent sharp jolts of pain coursing through his body with every upward pull. Yet, he climbed, driven by a force that melded the need to conquer this mountain and a deep, personal challenge to himself.

At this moment, Jason's existence distilled to its purest form, each sensation heightened and intertwined with the rawness of his injuries. The rock's rough texture was now grating against his tender skin, and every contact was a mixture of determination and discomfort. The wind's sharp sting was no longer just a slap against his face but a balm to the heat of his abrasions. The earthy scent of stone and soil, mingled with the metallic hint of his blood, filled his senses, grounding him in the moment. There was beauty here, amidst this dance with danger, a beauty that was as raw and pure as the pain and the exhilaration of his perilous ascent.

Without warning, fate indiscriminately chose to strike. Jason's damaged fingers, already compromised, faltered. Suddenly, he was falling. Time stretched and contorted, transforming seconds into lifetimes as he plummeted toward the unforgiving earth below. His life didn't flash before his eyes; instead, there was a heightened awareness, a vivid consciousness of his descent. The rush of wind was a roar in his ears, the world a blur of colors spinning wildly around him.

Instinctively, Jason reacted. Driven by a primal urge to survive, he grappled desperately at the cliff as he fell. Each fleeting contact with the jagged face slowed his descent. His body sawed against the mountain's harsh surface. The abrasions multiplied as he struggled against the inevitable. Yet, in those harrowing moments, suspended between life and death, an odd sense of peace enveloped him. It was as if the sheer intensity of the fall had stripped away all complexities, leaving only the raw, undeniable truth of his mortality. Visions of the mountains, the rivers, and the open skies of his youth intermingled with the realities of war-torn landscapes he had once navigated. His life of survival and an unyielding connection to the wild played out in his mind, not as thoughts or memories but as the essence of his very being.

The ground rushed to meet him, an unforgiving

welcome back to reality. And then, just as suddenly as it had begun, everything was black. The sensations, the sounds, and the pain—ceased instantly, leaving only silence and darkness in their wake.

In this void, suspended between chapters of his life, Jason's fate hung in the balance, a question left unanswered as the world faded away.

CHAPTER 2

The Solitary Life

Jason Masters' boots crunched on the rugged trail, each step echoing the solitude he had come to embrace. He stood atop the crest of a towering mountain, his gaze sweeping across the vast expanse below. Miles of open plains stretched out, uninterrupted by the buzz of modern life. It was the second day of his solitary excursion into the wilderness, a ritual that brought him closer to a world he understood, away from one that bewildered him.

The landscape before him was a picturesque frame of nature's untamed beauty. The plains rolled like waves, a dance of shadows and light playing across their surfaces as the sun dipped in the sky. In the distance, a herd of deer grazed peacefully, mere specks of life amidst the vastness. Above, the sky was a canvas of deepening blues and purples, the first stars of the evening beginning to twinkle in the twilight.

Jason inhaled deeply, the crisp mountain air filling his lungs. It was rich with the scent of pine needles and the faint, earthy aroma of damp soil. The wind whispered through the trees, a gentle hush that spoke of ancient times and secrets untold. It was a soothing sound that resonated deep within him, calming his restless spirit.

As he stood atop the world, the rough texture of the rock beneath his feet contrasted with the earth's soft give on the trail. He could feel the solidity of the mountain supporting him, a steady presence that had withstood the passage of time. This connection to the earth was grounding, as Jason felt part of the enduring cycle of life and nature's unyielding strength.

Jason's eyes traced the horizon, following the jagged outline of distant peaks against the sky. The setting sun cast a golden glow over the landscape, illuminating the world in a warm, amber light that transformed the ordinary into something extraordinary. The beauty of the scene was overwhelming. For a moment, Jason felt as if he were part of something much larger than himself, a small piece in the grand tapestry of the universe.

He closed his eyes, listening to the symphony of nature that surrounded him. The rustle of leaves, the distant call of a bird, the gentle babble of a stream somewhere far below—music that required no audience yet filled the soul with a profound peace. This was the world as it was meant to be, wild and free, and he was privileged to witness its majesty.

The taste of the mountain air was pure and invigorating, a subtle blend of pine and the cool freshness that heralded the approach of night. It was a taste that spoke of freedom, of a life untethered from the constraints of society. Jason savored it, letting it linger on his tongue to remind him why he had chosen this solitary path.

Far in the distance, nestled in the embrace of the plains, lay his parents' sprawling cattle farm. The Masters family had toiled these thousands of acres for generations, cultivating a life as resilient and enduring as the earth itself. With its grandeur and scope, the farm echoed the unwavering spirit of his father, a hardened man shaped by the land he cultivated. His mother, a local woman of simpler joys, found her world in the gardens and animals she nurtured.

Jason's life was one of solitude and introspection, deeply rooted in the sprawling landscapes of his childhood. On the family farm, his world was one of silent communication with the animals and the endless, open fields. He found solace in the company of cattle, understanding their silent language, a gift he naturally possessed but never fully embraced. It was as if he held a quiet rebellion against the life his father envisioned for him, a life tethered to the cycles of farming and livestock. His innate connection with animals was undeniable. Jason chose not to nurture this gift, seeking instead the solitude of the farm's furthest corners, where he could be alone with his thoughts.

In high school, Jason's presence was like a gentle breeze—felt but seldom noticed. Academically, he excelled without apparent effort, his mind effortlessly grasping concepts and ideas that others struggled to understand. Yet, his gaze was often drawn to the world outside the classroom window, toward the distant mountains and meandering rivers that called to his spirit. He was neither an outcast nor a part of the in-crowd, existing in a realm of his own making—a realm where he was content in his isolation.

Jason's reputation as a loner was cemented in eighth grade when his quiet strength and resolve were tested. When a couple of bullies cornered him for his lunch money, they quickly learned that his gentle demeanor belied a fierce spirit. The altercation was brief but decisive, with both bullies needing the nurse's care while Jason calmly sat down to finish his lunch. The incident became a silent marker of his character; he sought no trouble but was unafraid to end it. From then on, his peers treated him with a mix of respect and cautious distance.

This incident foreshadowed the man he would become—a man of quiet strength, unassuming yet unyielding when pushed. He drifted through his high school years like a shadow, there but unanchored to the social dramas and cliques that defined teenage life. His teachers often noted his potential, encouraging him to engage more with his peers and the world around him. But Jason remained an island, his thoughts and dreams anchored in the vast, untamed wilderness that stretched beyond the school's walls.

His relationship with his father during these years was a silent dance of mutual respect and unspoken disagreements. His father, a man whose life was as ingrained in the farm as the ancient oak that stood by the barn, had hoped Jason would follow in his footsteps. Jason's father recognized the distant look in his son's eyes, a look that spoke of a yearning for something beyond the fences of their land. Their conversations were often a series of implicit understandings, with words as sparse as rain in a drought.

Jason's mother watched her son's growing independence with a bittersweet heart. She saw his love for the solitude of nature, a trait she cherished in her own way through her gardens and the care of their animals. She often left him be, knowing that the rolling hills and open skies provided him a comfort she could not. She supported his silent quest for identity, hoping he would one day find his place in the world, whether on the farm or beyond the horizon.

As Jason neared the end of his high school

years, his life path began to take shape. The call of the wild, the allure of the unknown, beckoned him. The military seemed a natural progression for Jason Masters—a loner, a dreamer, and a seeker of his truth. It offered the needed structure and the adventure he craved.

After graduating high school at 17, he enlisted with his parents' blessing, stepping into a world far removed from his childhood's open fields and skies. The confines of boot camp were his first real test - the barracks and the base lacking the wilderness that had been his sanctuary. The rigid discipline. The close quarters. They chafed against his love for solitude and open spaces.

But even in this constricted environment, Jason's spirit couldn't be dimmed. He heard whispers of Ranger training—tales of its rigorous demands and how much of it was conducted in solitary wilderness conditions. This idea resonated with him, stirring the dreamer and the lone wolf within. He enthusiastically went to jump school after boot camp, setting his sights on the next challenge with a quiet determination that had always been his trademark.

In jump school, Jason's natural aptitude shone

through. His ease in adapting to airborne operations caught the eye of a Green Beret commander. Although a direct path to Ranger training wasn't immediately available, he was assigned to the 82nd Airborne Division, where he continued to excel. His time in the 82nd was marked by an overseas combat deployment, only served to hone his skills and deepen his resolve. His childhood, spent roaming the wilderness of his family's farm, had unwittingly prepared him for the rigors of military life in ways he could never have foreseen.

By the age of 21, his dream was realized. He found himself serving in a Ranger Battalion. His skills and dedication led him to multiple deployments in the Middle East. These years shaped and tempered him. The training was relentless, but to Jason, it felt like a continuation of his life's journey. The wilderness that had been his childhood playground was now his battlefield.

The most fulfilling part of his military career came in the latter half of his service when he was assigned to a reconnaissance team that utilized horses. His upbringing on the farm had made him a skilled rider, a trait that seamlessly integrated him into this new role. He relished the work. It was a return to his roots, traveling through rugged terrain on horseback with a small team that mirrored the close-knit community of his family.

These were the years that Jason felt most at home in the military. The vast, untamed landscapes of the Middle East, so different yet so similar to the plains and mountains of his youth, were where he could blend his soldier's discipline with his natural affinity for the wild. The solitary nature of reconnaissance, the bond with the horses, and the small, tight-knit team were as close to a sense of belonging as he had ever felt.

However, not all journeys have a clear path, and Jason's time in the military was cut short. A final battle, the details of about which he seldom spoke, led to his medical discharge after eleven years of dedicated service. He left the Army not as the boy who yearned for the mountains and rivers of his home but as a man etched with the marks of war, carrying experiences too profound and complex for simple words.

Now, Jason found himself retreating more into the embrace of nature, his sanctuary from a world he could no longer fully grasp. The Army, life, and the relentless drum of combat had profoundly affected him. In the wilderness, which had once been his playground and then his battleground, he sought solace—a refuge where the cacophony of his past was muted by the symphony of the wind and the rustle of leaves. Here, amidst the unjudging embrace of nature, he could escape the invisible yet heavy chains of PTSD, a condition he would not acknowledge but lived with every day.

His reintegration into civilian life was marred with challenges he hadn't foreseen. The ordinary flow of everyday life, the conversations, and the bustling crowds seemed alien to him. He felt disconnected, a wanderer between two worlds where he no longer belonged. People, their routines and concerns, appeared trivial against the backdrop of what he had experienced. This dissonance, this feeling of being perpetually out of place, made the solitude of nature not just a choice; it was a necessity for Jason. In the vast, open spaces, he found a brief respite from the struggle to reconnect with a life that once was.

Since returning, his life on the farm has been one of coexistence rather than integration. His stoic and understanding parents gave him space. They didn't press for conversation at the dinner table, nor did they intrude into the silence that was his constant companion. His father was a man of few words and communicated in shared tasks - repairing fences and tending to the cattle. Their conversations were the unspoken language of work and presence. His mother, a gentle soul, tried to reach out with small gestures—a plate of food left by his door, clean laundry folded neatly. They were tokens of love from a distance, respecting the invisible barrier he had erected around himself.

But in the mountains, Jason felt a sense of freedom. Here, the rules were simple, dictated by nature and necessity. He relished the challenge of living off the land, drawing on skills honed in a life that seemed distant and uncomfortably close. The wilderness was unforgiving, yet it was a straightforwardness he appreciated. Unlike people, the mountains and forests didn't mask their intentions or judge his inability to reconnect with a world he no longer felt a part of.

As the sun dipped below the horizon, it painted the sky in shades of fire and twilight. Jason peered in awe as he slowly set up his campsite. The simplicity of his actions, the building of a fire, and the setting up of a tent were meditative. In these moments, he found a peace that eluded him in the presence of others.

Amidst the whispering pines and under the vast canopy of stars, Jason allowed himself to reflect on the day, his chosen path, and the journey ahead. This solitary life was not one he had envisioned as a boy on the farm or a soldier in distant lands. It was the life he now navigated, one step at a time, finding solace in the rhythm of nature and the quiet understanding of the mountains.

Jason snugged himself in his bivy sack. He sat for a while, pondering life. His thoughts drifted to tomorrow's rigorous climb, a challenge that incited him since childhood. With a deep sigh, his body relaxed, and his head melted into the soft pillow. Here, beneath the expanse of the night sky, Jason felt whole. He forced his gaze to the Milky Way but finally surrendered to the weight of his eyelid.

CHAPTER 3

Military Forged

The sun had barely risen over the San Luis Valley as the taxi's engine faded into the distance. Jason Masters stood at the edge of his family's farm. The long driveway stretched before him. His eyes traced the contours of the landscape that had shaped much of his life. The familiar sight of the cattle grazing in the fields and the distant peaks of the Sangre de Cristo Mountains brought a sense of calm. It was a brief respite from the turmoil that often plagued his mind. Each step he took along the gravel path was a step back in time, his boots crunching in rhythm with the echoes of his past.

His mind drifted to boot camp, the first forging

of the soldier he had become. The rigors of basic training, discipline, and structure were similar yet divergent from the freedom of childhood. In the military's strict regimen, he found a new kind of freedom—a purpose and clarity that had eluded him.

Fort Benning, Georgia, is one of the primary locations for U.S. Army Basic Combat Training. There, Jason found himself immersed in a world far removed from his youth's open skies and mountains. The construct of boot camp was an intense fusion of physical rigor, mental discipline, and relentless training designed to break down individuality and rebuild a soldier. Days were long and grueling, filled with endless drills, marches, and exercises that tested the limits of endurance and willpower.

For Jason, boot camp was a challenge and an opportunity to excel. He directed his energies at mastering each task and each exercise with a single-minded focus. His striving wasn't to outdo his peers. It was to surpass his expectations. Each day was a personal dare, pushing himself beyond what he thought possible. Within the demands of training, Jason's resolve solidified. He learned to channel the independence and resilience fostered by his upbringing into the discipline and structure of military life.

His dedication did not go unnoticed. Jason quickly distinguished himself, not through a desire for recognition, but through his unwavering commitment to being the best soldier he could be. His efforts earned him accolades, but more importantly, they reaffirmed his belief in his capabilities. With its rigorous demands, boot camp laid the foundation for his military career, shaping him into a soldier defined by determination and self-discipline. This initial phase of his military journey was the first step in a transformative process defining his identity and path forward.

During basic training, Jason's gaze would often drift upwards, drawn to the sight of soldiers parachuting from C-130s against the thick Georgia sky. The thrill of the jump and the graceful descent of the parachutists sparked a yearning in him. His enlistment included a promise, an opportunity to attend jump school immediately following basic training, a prospect that filled him with anticipation.

After graduation from boot camp, Jason

transitioned to airborne training. The atmosphere was charged with a blend of excitement and apprehension. The days were intense, a rigorous blend of physical training, technical instruction, and practical exercises. He learned the mechanics of the parachute, the intricacies of jump procedures, and the art of landing safely. The trainers were seasoned veterans, their instructions laced with experience and authority. Jason absorbed every lesson and every detail, and his focus was unwavering. He relished the physical challenges, pushing himself to excel. But nothing compared to the moment of his first static line jump.

In the cramped, vibrating belly of the C-130, Jason sat with his fellow trainees, each clad in bulky jump gear. The aircraft's engines thundered, a backdrop to the heightened tension among the recruits. Jason's heart hammered against his chest, a syncopated rhythm that matched the nervous energy around him. His hands were clad in well-worn gloves as he gripped the static line—a lifeline in the literal sense. The anticipation was a tangible force, every soldier silently grappling with their thoughts with a mix of fear and exhilaration.

As the aircraft neared the jump point, the

jumpmaster's signal cut through the tension like a knife. A loud buzz cracked through the fuselage. The door swung open abruptly, and an invisible hand seemed to snatch the air from the cabin. The world outside was a maelstrom of sound and fury, the wind howling as it invaded the space, whipping around them in a frenzy. Jason's ears popped from the sudden decompression, a physical effect of the altitude and the task ahead. The world outside was a dizzying blue sky and distant earth, a canvas of freedom and fear. The drop zone was a small piece of the earth's puzzle far below. It seemed inviting but menacing.

The soldiers stood, promptly obeying the jumpmaster's commands. One by one, they disappeared, jumping through the menacing vortex of uncertainty and expectation. Jason's turn edged closer, each step forward a march toward destiny. His breaths came in short, measured gasps, a futile attempt to calm the storm within. As he stood at the edge, staring into the abyss, time seemed to slow. His mind raced with thoughts of past, present, and an uncertain future colliding in a whirlwind of emotion. The jumpmaster's shouts crashed his eardrums, "Go. Go. Go.!" He crossed the threshold with a steadying breath that tasted of oil and metal.

As Jason stepped into the abyss, it was as though he had crossed the threshold of reality into a realm of uncharted sensation. The instant his boots lost contact with the cargo deck, a visceral shockwave surged through his body. The world as he knew it dissipated as an overwhelming torrent of sensations assaulted him.

The air around him transformed into a living, breathing entity, howling with a ferocity that resonated to his core. Like a wild beast, it gripped him, tugging at his limbs, clothes, and very skin as if seeking to tear him asunder. Each gust was an icy claw, raking across his body, leaving trails of numbing cold in its wake. Jason was a solitary figure among many plummeting through chaos, a human comet streaking through an infinite azure canvas.

Below him, the earth was indiscernible—a distant blur of colors and shapes. Above, the sky stretched endless and unyielding, a vast dome of cerulean mystery. Jason was the epitome of insignificance, a fleeting, ephemeral presence in the grandeur of the cosmos.

His heart thundered in his chest, a wild, unrestrained rhythm that matched the tempo of his descent. Adrenaline coursed through his veins like liquid fire, igniting every nerve with electrifying intensity. Senses amplified, every sound a symphony, every gust a tempest, every heartbeat a drumroll in this thrilling dance with fate.

Snap. The static line cracked taut in an abrupt defiance against this unbridled freedom. It was a rude, jarring intrusion, yanking him back to the harsh reality of his descent. The parachute deployed with an assertive jerk, unfurling above him like the wings of a guardian angel. In a heartbeat, the chaotic descent morphed into a serene float, the previously roaring winds now a gentle whisper, cradling him in a protective embrace as he glided toward the earth.

This transition, from the raw ferocity of freefall to the tranquil drift under the canopy, was a journey of extremes. It encapsulated the essence of human resilience and vulnerability and the audacity of the human spirit to soar, even in the face of the unfathomable.

As he descended, the world transformed below him. The patchwork landscape gradually took shape—fields, roads, and rivers coming into focus. The sensation of floating, of being cradled by the sky, was exhilarating, a dance with gravity that was both terrifying and liberating. This first foray into the realm of Army Airborne was a moment of pure, unadulterated freedom—the answer to the human spirit's yearning to break free from the earth's hold. It was an experience etched into his soul, a memory that would forever symbolize his leap into the unknown.

Jason's descent culminated not in a textbook drop-and-roll landing but in a display of sheer fearlessness and exhilaration. His feet struck the ground with a force reverberating through his bones, yet he remained unyielding. Standing tall and unwavering in an upright run, he was a monument to the thrill of the jump.

His steps were not tentative but purposeful, charged with the adrenaline that still coursed through his veins. His voice erupted in a triumphant yell, "AIRBORNE! Oh, Yeah. Army Fucking Airborne!" The words sliced through the air, a fierce declaration of victory over the daunting leap he had just conquered.

Laughter spilled from him, unrestrained and

wild, echoing across the open field. It was laughter born from the euphoria of the experience, tinged with a hint of disbelief at his daring feat. Tears streamed down his face, not from fear or pain but from the overwhelming elation that bubbled within him. It was laughter that danced on the edge of mania, an intense emotional release after flirting so closely with the vast, unyielding sky.

Jason's landing was more than a physical return to earth; it was a triumphant assertion of life, a celebration of the human spirit's capacity for exhilaration and joy. With his laughter ringing out under the expanse of the sky, he was more than just a soldier who had completed a jump; he felt free and invincible.

Jason slowly shuffled his way down the stretching driveway. The ground, the dirt, it felt different here. It's more solid than the terrain of the East's Sandbox. His thoughts drifted to the renowned 82nd Airborne Division, his first duty station. Fort Bragg was a prestigious assignment. They were placing him among the elite. The 82nd was known for its storied history and role as a rapid deployment force, ready to respond to crises worldwide.

And it held to its name. Only weeks after being assigned, his unit deployed.

Jason's first deployment with the 82nd to the Middle East was pivotal in his military career. His division was actively involved in various missions around Iraq. Their role was advisory and training as part of the U.S. efforts to support Iraqi security forces in the fight against terror. His unit was instrumental in providing *advise-and-assist* support focusing on training, securing critical facilities, and offering logistical support to bolster Iraq's efforts against insurgents. The training extended to more complex collective tasks, preparing Iraqi forces for larger-scale operations. As part of these training teams, Jason found a deep sense of fulfillment in this work, witnessing the enthusiasm and trust of the Iraqi forces toward their American trainers.

During this deployment, a small unit of the 82nd was tasked to join a detachment of Army Rangers and U.S. Navy SEALs on specialized missions neutralizing terrorist sympathizers in the outer regions of the cities. These operations gave Jason his first real taste of combat, working alongside elite Rangers and SEALs. He was involved in several operations marked by direct combat and significant successes, including vital hostage extractions. During one such mission, Jason's bravery earned him a silver star.

The mission was a high-stakes hostage rescue deep in hostile territory. Jason's three-man 82nd unit was tasked with securing the *back door*—ensuring a safe extraction route for the SEALs. The mission was swift and precise; four SEALs infiltrated the enemy stronghold, successfully neutralizing the targets and retrieving the hostage. As they headed to Jason's position for extraction, the tension was palpable.

Unbeknownst, terrorist sympathizers had noticed them and set a deadly ambush along the extraction route. The enemy held the high ground on both sides of the road, hidden and ready to strike. As the SEALs engaged the enemy on one side, the 82nd soldiers confronted the other. The SEALs quickly neutralized their threat, but Jason's side faced a sniper and a heavy gun pinning them down.

In the chaos of the ambush, Jason's instincts took over. His teammate lay vulnerable, the sniper's lethal gaze fixed upon him. Time slowed as Jason processed the situation. He knew what he had to do. With a resolve forged in his Colorado youth, he surged forward, sprinting up the hillside.

Every step was a tango with destiny, his boots churning the dusty terrain as enemy fire tore through the air around him. Bullets cracked by, each one a whisper of mortality, but Jason's determination was unshakable. His breaths came in sharp, rapid bursts, the adrenaline coursing through him, fueling his ascent. The earth erupted beneath his feet, the enemy's attempts to cut him down only propelling him forward with greater urgency.

As he crested the hill, his surroundings narrowed to a tunnel of focus. The sniper, unaware of Jason's approach, was methodically taunting prey with searching plinks of death. In a fluid motion born of countless hours of hunting, training, and instinct, Jason slid to position, his rifle becoming an extension of his will. His finger squeezed the trigger. The shot rang with finality as the enemy sniper crumpled—the threat—extinguished.

But the battle was yet over. The heavy gun, its relentless fire moving between his position and pinning down the SEALs, was Jason's next target. He moved with a predator's grace, each crawl and step calculated to draw the gunner's attention. Darting from cover to cover, Jason became a phantom on the battlefield, his movements a blur of tactical precision. The enemy gunner, drawn by Jason's maneuvering, shifted focus, unleashing a hail of fire in his direction.

This was the moment the SEALs needed. With the heavy gun distracted, they sprang into action, their coordinated assault a lethal ballet of gunfire. The heavy weapon fell silent under their onslaught, the ambush broken, the path to safety now clear.

Jason made his way down the hill toward his comrades and the SEALs. As he breached the perimeter, one of the SEALs approached, "What's your name, boy?"

Jason sprung to attention, "Masters, Sir. Private first-class Jason Masters, 82nd Airborne division." Jason's response brought on wicks and chuckles from the other SEALs. The SEAL armed Jason as they walked to the injured soldier.

"That was some mighty fancy shit you just pulled there," the SEAL commented.

Another SEAL added, "Senior Chief, you sure he's not one of us?"

"Nah, he's too fucking skinny," was the jesting reply.

Jason could not help but join in the laughter. The Senior Chief SEAL slapped Jason one last time.

"Fucking impressive. I see Specialist and a Star in your future."

In the aftermath, as the dust settled and the echoes of battle faded, Jason's actions resonated deeply. His courage under fire and willingness to risk everything for his comrades was a defining moment in his military journey. This bravery and unwavering commitment to his brothers-in-arms would point him to Ranger Selection, cementing his destiny as a soldier of unparalleled valor and determination.

"Jason. Jason." His mother's calls brought him back to the moment. He kicked the dust off his boots and looked up. He couldn't help but smile as he embraced his mother. Her embrace was warm and lovingly strong. He could smell the fresh cooking. His pallet longed for the savory essence of his mother's culinary genius.

As they crossed the threshold of the home, Jason's father stood tall and proud with a telling shit-eating grin. His father held up a bottle, dusty but recognized.

"I told you I'd have this ready for when you came home."

CHAPTER 4

The Power of Will

Jason opened his eyes, the sun's harsh light piercing his blurred vision. He lay sprawled on the rugged ground, his body a canvas of pain and injury. His mind, clouded by a concussion, struggled to piece together the fragments of his fall from the cliff. Each breath was a labor, his cracked ribs protesting with sharp jabs of pain.

As Jason's consciousness slowly flickered back, his eyes locked on conifer branches swaying gently against the sky. Lying there, he puzzled over his survival, his mind grappling with the reality of the fall and the improbable mercy of his landing. The canopy above, a tangled lattice of pine, showed signs of his descent—a trail of broken branches, each a tell to how they had cushioned his fall, slowing his plummet to the earth.

Underneath him, the ground was unexpectedly forgiving. He could feel the softness, a natural cushion made of years' worth of pine needles, decayed undergrowth, and moss. This wasn't the hard, unyielding surface one would expect at such altitudes. It was as if this particular spot, nestled within the arms of the mountain, was purposefully made softer, more resilient. A mere twenty feet to either side, he would have met a different fate against the merciless boulders.

Lying there, Jason gazed through the natural skylight formed by the trees, his mind tracing the broken path he had carved through their branches. It was a chaotic and oddly graceful map of his descent—a series of fortunate interruptions that had spared him from the full brutality of the fall. The pine-scented air filled his lungs as he took in the serenity of his surroundings, but the violence of his tumble was evident.

Pain seared through every part of his body as he tried to hold consciousness. This sensation was not unfamiliar to Jason. It transported him back to the rugged terrains of the North Georgia mountains during the grueling mountain phase of Ranger School. Jason found a strange sense of belonging among the towering pines and jagged cliffs. He thrived in the rigorous training, his body and mind attuned to the unforgiving wilderness.

The mountain phase was designed to test physical and mental limitations. It was a relentless trial of endurance, navigation, and leadership under extreme conditions. Jason, a natural in this environment, often led the team through the dense forests and rugged peaks. His understanding of the terrain and innate leadership skills stood out among his peers.

One incident in particular stood out in Jason's memory. During a treacherous night navigation exercise, a fellow recruit, Private Martinez, slipped and suffered a severe leg injury. Isolated and hours away from any medical assistance, the situation was dire. Without hesitation, Jason took charge. He quickly fashioned a splint from his rucksack frame and used his survival skills to stabilize Martinez's injury. His calm demeanor and swift action inspired confidence in his team.

What followed was a show of Jason's strength

and determination. He carried Private Martinez on his back, leading his team through the perilous terrain. Every step was a battle against exhaustion and the elements, but Jason's resolve never wavered. His connection with the natural world around him seemed to give him an almost superhuman endurance.

Those long hours trekking through the mountains, with the weight of a fellow soldier on his back, did not just shape Jason; it was part of his core. The mountains' harsh beauty and unforgiving nature perfectly mirrored Jason's spirit. In the face of adversity, he found his true self. Jason felt alive during Ranger School. Each challenge and each obstacle he overcame brought him closer to understanding his true capabilities. The mountain phase was more than a training ground; it strengthened the depth of his resilience and the unyielding power of his will.

With immense effort, he turned his head, noticing the scattered content of his backpack. The sight sparked a flicker of hope. But his broken leg and dislocated shoulder anchored him to the cruel reality. He knew he had to move to reach his campsite, where a slightly higher percentage of salvation lay in food, water, and basic medical supplies. It was 75 yards away, but it might as well have been in New Hampshire, given his condition.

As he contemplated his next move, the pain surged through his body, sending him spiraling into unconsciousness. In these moments of darkness, memories of his military life flashed before him. The rigors of being a Ranger, the adrenaline of combat, the bonds forged in war—all danced in his mind's eye.

One eerily familiar memory stood out as he lay there. A vivid, almost déjà vu, memory of an accident that nearly sidelined him from Ranger School. It was during the infamous "Swamp School," as Jason affectionately called it. The Florida phase of the course is known for its brutal and unforgiving nature.

The day began with helicopter insertions into the dense swamps, a critical start to their solo navigation exercises. The chopper had roared above the swamp, buffeted by strong winds. It hovered just above the ground, the trainees poised to fast-rope down into the murky bogs below. Jason had been ready, his focus unwavering. But the mission took a violent turn.

The helicopter caught in a sudden gust and lurched sideways. Another Ranger trainee lost his footing, falling into Jason, sending them both tumbling out of the chopper. Jason hit the swamp first, the other recruit's weight crashing down on him, driving him deeper into the muck. The impact was brutal; he felt a sharp, agonizing jolt in his shoulder—it had dislocated upon impact. The chopper hovered. The Sergeant First Class Ranger Instructor peered downward, looking for the OK signal.

The other recruit quickly looked up, giving two pats on his head and the OK signal. Jason knew the stakes. Admitting to the injury would mean the end of his journey to becoming a Ranger. With the chopper looming, Jason gave the OK signal. The chopper quickly ascended, disappearing into the sky, leaving Jason and the other recruit in the isolated expanse of the swamp. Dazed but unharmed, his peer promptly gathered himself and vanished into the glade, leaving Jason alone with his pain.

Jason made his way out of the bog and found a dry, secluded spot. Gritting his teeth against the pain, he reset the dislocated shoulder. The pain was blinding, a searing, white-hot agony that coursed through his entire body. But he pushed through, driven by sheer will and determination.

After the excruciating procedure, Jason allowed himself to rest and gather his strength. His shoulder throbbed painfully, but he couldn't let that stop him. He knew he had to complete the navigation track; failure was not an option.

Drawing on his deep reservoir of resilience, Jason set out on his path, each step bringing him closer to his Ranger tab.

The memory brought a surge of determination. If he had overcome that, he could overcome this. With gritted teeth, he braced himself against the ground, preparing to reset his dislocated shoulder. The pain was piercing, a searing fire that coursed through his nerves. He pushed through it, fueled by the will to survive.

The first attempt failed, sending him back into the abyss of unconsciousness. But Jason was not one to yield. Each blackout, each surge of pain, was met with renewed persistence. Finally, with a guttural cry, he managed to reset the shoulder. The pain was overwhelming, yet it was accompanied by triumph and release. He lay there momentarily, gathering his strength, his eyes fixated on the distant campsite. It was more than just a destination; it symbolized his indomitable spirit. Before he could move, he needed to splint his leg. Rest, he thought. For now, he just needed to rest.

Thoughts of the Army were a continuous stream. Discipline, resilience, and sheer willpower had been his allies. These qualities had defined him as a soldier; now, they were his lifelines. Jason's journey in the military was more than a series of physical challenges; it was a constant exercise of willpower, in line with Huxley's assertion of the human capacity for self-determination and strength of mind.

He reflected on a pivotal mission long buried in the recesses of his mind. Under a scorching sun in a distant land, his unit navigated through a narrow pass. The air was thick with tension as they unwittingly walked into an ambush. The earth erupted around them, dust and sound swirling in a maddening dance. Seconds stretched as time slowed. Jason's clarity emerged like a silhouette against the chaos. It was becoming a noticeable part of his battle persona, the ability to become something more than himself—primitive yet intelligently aware.

In battle, there is no space for fear, only the

raw, unspoken understanding of what needs to be done. Jason's orders were crisp, slicing through the din like a blade. Each movement and decision birthed something deeper—a primal assertion of the will to exist against the odds. His actions that day earned him more military accolades. Jason did not covet these honors. His spirituality existed in experiences and the unfolding of the untapped human capacity.

Jason's memory drifted to another mission. Under a moonless sky, his team crept through shadowed terrain toward the objective. The mission was a whisper, a ghost of an aim that hung over them like a shroud. That night, the darkness was a veil, and they were the unseen artists, painting their path with silent precision. In the unity of their purpose, in the unspoken bond of their brotherhood, there was a powerful affirmation of their collective will, subtle yet as tangible as the weapons they bore. This mission, distinct from the turmoil of the ambush, was an exercise in the art of invisibility, defined by its delicacy, silence, and the imperative to leave no trace. In their juxtaposition in process and action, these two missions together serve as a Rosetta Stone, unlocking a deeper understanding of the versatile nature of his character and the tenacity and discipline of Jason Masters.

When the world is reduced to the immediacy of survival, Jason finds an unspoken truth. It's not just about the battles he fought on the outside; it's equally about the ones he conquered within. His journey is a silent ode to the power of the human spirit, an unyielding will that thrives in the face of life's relentless challenges.

As rested as possible, Jason found the strength to bind a makeshift splint to his leg. With deft, practiced hands, he fashioned the splint from branches, strips of his shirt, and his backpack. Each movement was deliberate despite the pain. The splint was rudimentary but sturdy—borne from a resourcefulness honed in countless challenging situations. Securing it tightly, he felt a wave of relief as it provided some stability. This was a physical anchor reinforcing his determination. Alas, the long creep started.

With every excruciating crawl and laborious drag toward the campsite, Jason Masters felt the weight of his past – a mosaic of military experiences – pressing upon him. Each inch gained was a victory over the searing pain that threatened to consume his resolve. His breaths were sharp and ragged, cutting through the stillness of the wilderness like a blade. The ground beneath him, uneven and unforgiving, became his adversary, challenging every move.

The world around him blurred into a kaleidoscope of pain and determination. The trees, once mere sentinels of nature, now seemed to loom over him, witnessing his struggle. The rustling leaves whispered tales of resilience while the earthy scent of the forest filled his senses, grounding him in the here and now. His hands, caked with dirt and sweat, became instruments of his will, clawing at the earth with a primal urgency.

Every painful inch forward was a re-living of past battles—the relentless training, the deafening roars of combat, the silent nights on foreign soil. These memories cascaded through his mind, not as mere reminiscences but as fuel for his indomitable spirit. In the symphony of his aching body, he heard echoes of gunfire, of commands shouted over the chaos, of the solemn silence that followed victory. "Hold on," he told himself. He knew another blackout could be his last slip into nothingness.

His mind, a fortress of discipline, refused to yield to the agony. Instead, it painted a picture of the soldier he had become—unbreakable, relentless, a survivor. Each grueling movement, each groan defying limitations, each pause a strategy to gather strength.

Though personal and isolated, this journey was no less a battle than those he had faced with his comrades. Here, in the solitude of nature, Jason was waging a war against his own body's betrayal, against the creeping tendrils of doubt and the lurking shadows of defeat, of death. But surrender was a word long erased from his lexicon.

Now a clearer vision in the outstretch, the campsite beckoned him with the promise of rest and safety. Yet, for Jason, it was more than a destination; it embodied his unyielding resolve, a beacon of hope amid his ordeal. Each drag a step further from defeat.

As the sun descended, casting long shadows over the land, Jason Masters, the soldier, the survivor, the indomitable spirit, reached his Mecca. Jason burst out with histrionic emotion as his unfurled fingers caressed the side of the welcoming tent.

CHAPTER 5

Survive

Jason Masters awakened in his bivy, each breath a sharp reminder of his precarious situation. He lay still for a moment, the pain throbbing through his body like a persistent drumbeat. Slowly, he sat up, his movements cautious and deliberate. Surveying his supplies, he realized the gravity of his plight. Medical supplies were sufficient for the most basic care, and the food and water would last about a day.

This was a familiar dance with mortality, yet different from his brushes with death in combat. There, he had the camaraderie of fellow soldiers, the immediacy of danger shared. Here, in the solitary embrace of nature, the enemy was his battered body, the silence of the wilderness, and the relentless march of time.

Usually a fortress of resolve, his mind wavered as he contemplated his chances. The distension in his abdomen was a silent alarm signaling possible internal bleeding. If his fears were valid, his time was measured in hours, not days. He had to move and attempt the arduous journey back to civilization.

With a grimace etched deep on his weathered face, Jason painstakingly fortified his ribcage, wrapping it tightly with a self-adherent bandage. The fabric compressed his chest and clung to his skin, constricting and fortifying his mid-section. Each inhale was a sharp stab of pain, but he endured, knowing the necessity of this crude armor.

His hands were trembling slightly from exertion and pain as he worked methodically to reinforce the splint on his broken leg. He gathered branches, his fingers moving with an almost mechanical precision born of countless hours of training and real-world survival scenarios. The splint was a resourcefulness symbol of the severity of his situation.

As he prepared to embark on the journey,

Jason's mind was acutely aware of the Herculean task ahead. With his leg now immobilized and his movements severely restricted, every step promised to be an ordeal of its own. The once-familiar act of walking had become a complex choreography of pain management and sheer determination.

He paused, steeling himself against the impending onslaught of pain that he knew would accompany his first movements. With a deep, shaky breath, he attempted to rise. His balance, betrayed by the rigidity of the splint and the constraints of his injuries, faltered. Jason stumbled, a sharp cry escaping his lips as he fell back to the ground, the impact sending a tsunami of agony through his body.

Sharp jolts of pain radiated from his broken ribs, echoing through his torso with a merciless intensity. The splint on his leg felt like a vise, gripping him with an unnatural stiffness that turned every attempt at movement into a harrowing ordeal.

Gritting his teeth, Jason prepared to try again. Once he managed to stand, his initial steps were tentative and awkward, each a precarious dance with pain. The rigid and unyielding splint forced him into an uneven gait, transforming what was once a simple act of walking into a complex, excruciating endeavor. With every step, the pain in his leg throbbed relentlessly, a counterpoint to the sharp stabs in his chest. His body screamed for respite, but he pushed through, driven by an unwavering determination to survive.

Once a place of solace and peace, the wilderness around him now felt like an endless, hostile expanse. The ground beneath him was no longer just the forest floor; it was an unpredictable terrain of obstacles. Each root was a potential snare, every rock a merciless impediment. With each painstaking step, he defied his physical limits, pushed through the engulfing tide of pain, and clung fiercely to his resolve to survive. His body, broken and battered, was driven by a spirit that refused to yield.

The wilderness greeted him with its indifferent and raw beauty—differing significantly from his internal struggle. The trek down the mountain was laborious, each step a calculated effort to minimize pain. His mind wandered to his first brush with death, the memories vivid against the backdrop of his current struggle.

Jason's ranger unit found themselves in a

perilous situation, confined within a small, dilapidated building. Surrounded by enemy forces, an intense firefight ensued. With only four men in his unit against multiple aggressors, the situation was dire. Their exit plan was clear: make it to the roof to be extracted by helicopter. However, with hostile forces positioned strategically above and below them, their predicament felt like a tightening snare.

Amid the tense standoff, the situation escalated dramatically. An enemy-fired rocket pierced through an open window. The building, already showing signs of structural damage, could not endure the impact. The floor gave way under the force of the explosion, sending Jason tumbling down through the collapsing structure. The fall was brutal; he was pummeled by falling debris, resulting in multiple injuries—broken ribs, a badly sprained ankle, and a fractured hand.

In the chaotic aftermath of the collapse, with his team engaged above and the enemy advancing, Jason found himself dazed but alive. Despite the pain and disorientation, he realized he was now behind the enemy. Driven by survival instinct and the training ingrained in him, Jason acted. In an almost desperate move, he ambushed the unsuspecting enemy from behind. Fueled by adrenaline and tactical acumen, this act was not a display of superheroic combat but a gritty, close-quarters Hail Mary struggle for survival. His unexpected counterattack provided the crucial diversion his team needed. Rallying their remaining strength and resources, they fought through the besieged building. Against all odds, they reached the roof, where the helicopter offered them a narrow, harrowing escape from what had seemed like inevitable defeat.

The sun traced its arc across the sky, and the hours stretched into an endless march for Jason. With each passing moment, his thoughts spiraled further into the depths of uncertainty and despair. The pain was unbearable, but it was the mental torment that was proving to be the most intolerable. The pressing question that loomed in his mind was inescapable: Would he make it through in time, or was this unforgiving wilderness destined to be the final chapter of his story?

Jason found himself strangely at peace with the notion of dying there. It seemed fitting, in a way. The wilderness had always been his refuge, where he felt most at home, away from the complexities and demands of human relationships. For Jason, who had dedicated his life to the disciplined and demanding world of the military, the idea of his final moments being in the embrace of nature was not a source of fear but of a certain solemn acceptance.

Yet, as he pondered this possibility, his thoughts turned to his parents. Their enduring love for each other, a constant backdrop to his life, began to stir something within him. It was the depth and resilience of their bond that made him pause. Jason had always observed their relationship from a distance, never fully engaging with the emotional intricacies that came with such a deep connection.

As he contemplated the reality of his situation, he began to see their love in a new light. It made him wonder about the facets of life he might have missed or overlooked. For the first time, he considered that there might be more to life than his disciplined, solitary existence. Maybe, just maybe, there was room for the kind of love and companionship he saw in his parents' lives.

This realization didn't alter his acceptance of his potential fate in the wilderness. Instead, it added a layer of introspection to his journey. Each step he took was not just a physical battle against the rugged terrain and his injuries but an inner exploration of what might have been and what could still be. As he moved forward, his thoughts oscillated between the serene acceptance of his situation and a newfound curiosity about the unexplored possibilities of human connection and love.

The fading light of the day cast sorrowful shadows across the forest, mirroring the turmoil in Jason's heart. Each step was a monumental effort, his body screaming in protest, every muscle and sinew strained to their limits. The forest felt like an endless labyrinth, its beauty lost to his pain-blurred eyes. His water was gone, his throat parched like the cracked earth beneath him. Exhaustion clawed at him, dragging him down with each labored step.

As the forest opened up, revealing grassy clearings ahead, Jason knew he was still far from safety. The realization was crushing, yet he trudged on, driven by a stubborn, dwindling flame of hope. The sun dipped lower, painting the sky in hues of fire and blood, mirroring the day's merciless toll on his body and spirit.

Jason needed to rest; his body was at its breaking point. Collapsing against a cold, unyielding rock,

Jason's gaze fell listlessly to the ground. That's when he saw it. Yarrow. In his near-delirious state, it took a moment for the significance to register. Yarrow—the warrior's herb, a beacon of healing in a sea of agony. Its presence here felt like a slight, merciful nod from the universe.

In his youth, he had learned of wild Yarrow's powers. Indigenous peoples and soldiers of old used it to stem bleeding and to reduce pain and inflammation. With its tiny, resilient white flowers, this humble plant was a lifeline thrown to him in his darkest hour. It was more than a plant; it symbolized survival, a natural remedy to soothe some of his physical torment.

As Jason gingerly gathered the Yarrow, he felt more assured and a little calmer. Then, the faint sound of trickling water teased his ears. A stream. A lifeline in the relentless wilderness. He dragged himself, clawing his way, each movement an act of sheer will. Alas, the cool water on his parched lips was like a kiss of life, reviving his flagging spirits and rekindling the flame of his will to survive. With this renewed zeal, he gathered some kindling and started a small warming fire.

The world around him dimmed as night

descended, enveloping him in its silent embrace. His body was a landscape of pain, yet Jason found a fragile peace with the Yarrow and the water's blessing. He leaned back against the rock and sipped on the warm yarrow tea, the realities of his plight weaving a heavy veil around him. Sleep, when it came, was a fitful respite, filled with the echoes of his struggles and the faint, lingering hope of a new day.

CHAPTER 6

The Mustang's Plight

Dawn breached the rugged landscape, casting a soft, golden light over the wilderness. Jason Masters, having survived the night, slowly stirred from his bivy sack. Though aching and battered, his body felt somewhat rejuvenated by the Yarrow's healing touch and the much-needed rest. He eyed his surroundings, the trickling stream nearby offering both a water supply and a path to follow. Despite his injuries, his spirit, fueled by thoughts of survival and a newfound introspection, remained unbroken.

As he resumed his arduous journey, every step was one of a resilient will. The wilderness seemed like an indifferent observer to his struggle, but Jason was driven by an unwavering tenacity. He pressed forward, his mind oscillating between the reality of his plight and reflective thoughts about life and connection.

Amid his laborious trek, Jason's attention was suddenly drawn to a distant figure. Initially, it appeared as a mere speck against the vast canvas of wilderness. Still, as he squinted against the sharp glare of the morning sun, the form began to take shape. Intrigued, he adjusted his path slightly, his curiosity piqued. With all its unpredictability, the wilderness had taught him to be wary, yet something about this figure beckoned him.

As he moved closer, the details started to emerge more clearly. It was an animal, large and majestic, yet something was amiss. The grace and freedom one would associate with a creature of the wild were replaced by a scene of struggle and desperation. Jason's steps quickened, driven by a concern that was surprising even to himself.

It was a horse, a wild Mustang, distinguished by its proud stature and the untamed mane that fluttered in the wind. But this noble creature was in distress. Its body was ensnared in coils of barbed wire, cruelly binding it, with a large piece of a fence post lodged, effectively trapping it in place. The wire dug into its flesh at places, painting a picture of pain and helplessness.

Jason's heart clenched at the sight. He had always maintained a neutral stance regarding horses, viewing them more as symbols of a life he had never fully embraced back on the farm. But now, seeing this wild creature in such a plight, a surge of compassion washed over him. The Mustang's eyes, wide with fear and pain, met his own, and in that gaze, Jason saw a reflection of his struggles, his battles with the invisible barbs of life.

The Mustang's coat was marred with streaks of red. The sight of the animal, so powerful yet so vulnerable, struggling against the confines of the wire and the weight of the fence post evoked an unexpected urging in Jason to help. It was a moment that transcended his past experiences and beliefs about horses, tapping into a vast well of empathy he hadn't realized he possessed.

He approached cautiously, mindful of the Mustang's pain and the potential danger of the barbed wire. Each step he took was measured, his eyes never leaving the Mustang. Their roles were reversed; the wild Mustang was cornered and in need, and Jason, a man who had often sought solace in isolation, was reaching out.

The Mustang grew tense with Jason's approach, its eyes flickering between fear and a faint glimmer of hope. Jason knew he had to tread carefully to avoid spooking the animal and prevent further harm to himself. He spoke in a low, soothing tone, a skill he had learned watching his father on the farm, using his voice to convey calm and reassurance.

The Mustang before Jason was a stunning embodiment of untamed nature. A stallion, rugged and robust, its coat brushstrokes of rich, earthy hues. Deep browns interspersed with streaks of black that shimmered under the sun's early light. Its mane was a wild cascade of dark strands, flowing with a life of its own, echoing the unbridled spirit that defined its very essence. Muscles rippled beneath its skin with each tense movement, showcasing a powerful physique honed by a life of freedom in the wilderness. Its eyes, deep and observant, sparkled with a willful intelligence, reflecting an unyielding desire for independence. This trait resonated deeply with Jason.

Jason saw a mirror of himself in this majestic creature, the strength and resilience, the rugged individualism, and the independent soul. Both were creatures of the wild, molded by their environments, survivors in landscapes that demanded toughness and adaptability. The Mustang, with its imposing presence, was a living symbol of the wild's heart - fierce, free, and undaunted. Its stance was commanding, an unspoken tribute to its authority over its domain, much like Jason, who had navigated his challenges with a similar blend of strength and hardiness.

There was a cautious kinship between them, a recognition of similar spirits carved from the same cloth of endurance and survival. The stallion's willful nature and refusal to yield despite adversity mirrored Jason's journey through life's trials. In the Mustang, Jason saw not just a wild animal but a reflection of his journey, a kindred spirit walking a parallel path. However, the anthropomorphic comparison did not cloud Jason's objectivity. He was acutely aware of the uncertainty, the potential for mutual benefit, and the risk of reciprocal detriment.

As Jason approached, the reality of the

Mustang's plight unfurled with a visceral intensity. The barbed wire, a ruthless human creation, had trapped the creature in its relentless grasp. It cruelly bit into the Mustang's flesh as blood oozed and dripped in a slow, macabre dance. The sharp barbs, rusted and unyielding, had lacerated the skin, leaving behind deep, gruesome wounds that were raw and inflamed, telling a silent story of the Mustang's frantic struggles for freedom.

Now part of this grim tableau, the fence post acted as an indomitable mooring. It was a grotesque appendage that trailed alongside the Mustang, its weight a constant, unrelenting force that cruelly reminded the animal of its failed attempts to escape. The post had torn patches of hide and mane, leaving ragged strips of hair entangled in the splintered wood and rusted wire. Each movement of the Mustang was a study in agony, the post scraping against the ground, reopening wounds, and etching new ones.

The Mustang's eyes, once bright with the fire of the untamed, now flickered with a mix of pain and resignation. Each inhale was a struggle against the pain that wracked its body. Powerful muscles, built for running free across the plains, twitched involuntarily, spasming from the trauma inflicted by the rusted wire and splintering post.

Around the Mustang, the ground was disturbed, a telltale of a desperate battle. The earth was churned up, hoofprints interspersed with dark smears of blood. Clumps of fur and flesh, harshly ripped from the Mustang's body, lay scattered about. It had endured a primal and brutal ordeal. The iron tang of blood floated in the air, mingling with the earthy scent of the wilderness.

This scene before Jason was a tragic mishap and a heart-wrenching symbol of the clash between the wild's untamed beauty and the unforgiving intrusions of human encroachments. The Mustang's raw injuries were a powerful indictment of this clash, a vivid portrayal of the struggle and suffering inflicted upon nature by the heedless advance of civilization.

Jason's mind, usually so focused on survival and his inner demons, now engulfed in a wave of empathy for the creature before him. He realized that their struggles, though different in nature, were similar in essence. They both were fighting against unforeseen constraints, a battle for freedom and survival. This moment of connection with the

Mustang was a powerful reminder of the broader struggles all living beings face.

He continued to speak softly, his voice a steady, calming presence in the quiet of the wilderness. His words were not just meant for the Mustang but also served as a balm to his soul, soothing the inner turmoil that had plagued him since his return from the military. This rescue was not just about the Mustang but also a healing process for Jason.

With each guarded step, Jason felt the weight of the responsibility he was about to undertake. He was no stranger to challenging situations, but this was different. Here, in the heart of nature, he was about to engage in a silent dialogue of trust with a wild animal. The Mustang, with its instinctive wariness of humans, would need to sense his intentions to understand that the help it needed was at hand.

As Jason cautiously attempted to approach the wounded Mustang, his movements were hindered by physical limitations. With a splinted, broken leg, each step was a calculated gamble in agility and endurance. The wild and unpredictable Mustang seemed to perceive his approach as a threat. Despite his best efforts to convey a sense of calm, the horse's instincts were on high alert, its survival reaction triggered by the perceived danger.

Jason slowly edged closer, attentive and watchful. In one heart-stopping moment, the Mustang lashed out. Its powerful hind legs kicked in a defensive maneuver, startling Jason. He lost his balance, falling backward awkwardly, the impact jarring his broken leg, sending a searing pain coursing through him. Lying on the ground, he couldn't help but recognize the irony of the situation - his intention to help was perceived as predatory, a threat in the eyes of this wild creature.

Jason lay there catching his breath. As he grappled with the pain, his mind drifted back to his childhood. He remembered his father, a man of few words but many lessons, who had tried to teach him the principles of natural horsemanship. His father had always emphasized the importance of understanding the predator-prey relationship in building a connection with horses. "You have to think like they do, see the world from their eyes," his father would say. These lessons, which Jason had once dismissed, now came flooding back with newfound relevance.

Jason recalled how his father had moved

around horses, always mindful of their space and perception, his movements deliberate yet non-threatening. He remembered the talks about building trust and how horses, as prey animals, were always vigilant, always reading intentions in the actions of others, especially predators. It dawned on Jason that his direct approaches, however well-intentioned, were akin to predator behavior in the eyes of the Mustang.

Jason realized he needed to recalibrate his approach. He began to draw upon what his father had taught him. He needed to communicate not with words but through behavior that conveyed trustworthiness and respect for the Mustang's space. It was about becoming less of a threat and more of a benign presence. He shifted his tactics, adopting a more indirect approach, avoiding direct eye contact, which could be perceived as a threat or challenge, and keeping his body language passive and non-threatening.

Jason understood this was just the beginning of a slow, patience-testing process. Building trust with a wild, injured animal was not a task that could be rushed. It required time, patience, and understanding of the animal's psyche. Lying there, he prepared himself for a long and cautious attempt at communication—a connection that would hopefully lead to a bond of trust between them. This was not just about rescuing the horse anymore; it was about connecting with it, about bridging the gap between man and wild through the silent, powerful language of mutual respect and understanding.

Jason spent the rest of the day in a delicate dance of proximity and patience with the Mustang, each movement steeped in forced remembering of lessons he once overlooked. He moved with mindful intention, echoing the quiet presence his father had always embodied. "Horses don't respond to you," his father's voice echoed in his memory, "They respond to your behaviors and your perceived intent." These words guided Jason's every step and breath as he sought to build a bridge of trust with the wild creature.

His movements were a deliberate counterpoint to the Mustang's wary shifts. He advanced not in a straight line but in gentle arcs, mimicking the non-confrontational approach of a fellow grazer rather than a predator. Each step was measured, his body language open yet unimposing, seeking to communicate a sense of safety and companionship. With flicks of its ears and tentative glances, the horse began to mirror Jason's calm. A silent conversation was developing between them. It was a delicate balance of giving space and slowly encroaching upon the invisible boundaries set by the Mustang.

In a moment of overconfidence, Jason, buoyed by the progress, misjudged the delicate equilibrium. He moved a fraction too swiftly, his hand reaching out to touch the Mustang's neck in a gesture he intended as comforting. The suddenness of his movement broke the spell. The horse, its instincts of a prey animal still finely tuned, perceived the abrupt gesture as a threat. The Mustang instantly recoiled, its powerful body knocking Jason back. He fell, the breath knocked out of him, an excruciating reminder of his physical vulnerability and the fragile nature of the trust he was attempting to forge.

As Jason lay there again, winded and staring up at the vast expanse above, he realized the depth of his father's teachings. Trust with a creature as intuitive and sensitive as a horse was not earned through haste or force but through consistent, respectful behavior and a deep understanding of their perception of the world. It was a lesson learned in the hardest way, lying on the ground, gasping for air, under the watchful eye of the Mustang he sought to help.

As Jason lay still in these quiet moments of recovery, something shifted in the dynamic between man and beast. The Mustang sensed Jason's vulnerability and passive intent and cautiously stepped closer. It was a gentle, inquisitive approach devoid of the earlier tension. With a soft nuzzle to Jason's shoulder, the Mustang bridged the gap that Jason's hasty movement had widened. As Jason slowly raised his hand, the Mustang allowed the contact, accepting his touch on its neck. It was a small victory in their evolving ballet of trust. It highlighted the bond that can emerge from genuinely listening to and respecting the innate nature of these majestic creatures.

Night captured the sky, moonless with vibrant pins of flickering light from galaxies afar. Jason and the Mustang cautiously continued their dance of trust. As the night darkened, the weight of exhaustion enticed Jason into an uneasy slumber. The Mustang stood alert, vigilantly watching over his every breath.

CHAPTER 7

Unlikely Companions

Jason woke to the labored, rhythmical breathing of the Mustang. Only feet away, it stood precariously close. Jason Masters found himself caught in a moment of profound introspection. His gaze locked onto the wild Mustang entangled in barbed wire, its struggles a bleak metaphor for his internal battles. The Mustang's eyes, wide with fear and pain, mirrored Jason's haunted memories of combat and the invisible scars of PTSD. But there was also something else in the Mustang's eyes. Curiosity and willingness. As the sun's filtered rays reached through the lingering morning mist, Jason held his breath as he approached the distressed animal.

Jason moved with a deliberateness that was almost ceremonial. Each step was a culmination of the wisdom ingrained in him by his father. The Mustang, a magnificent creature of the wild, remained vigilant, its muscles taut like coiled springs, ready to strike out at the slightest provocation.

The air between them was charged with an electric tension, a silent conversation of cautious curiosity and mutual wariness. Jason's eyes, reflecting determination and compassion, looked past the Mustang as if it were of no consequence. But Jason noted each flicker of the ear, twitch of skin, lip movement, swish of the tail, and shifting weight. He remembered his father's words, "Observe their language, son. Horses speak in whispers and subtle gestures. Listen with your eyes, speak with your presence."

Inching closer, Jason extended a hand, not as a gesture of domination but as an offering of peace, a symbol of shared vulnerability. He recalled his father's lessons on predator-prey dynamics, the importance of projecting calmness, and the significance of non-threatening body language. His father had often said, "In their world, every intention speaks louder than words. Be mindful, be gentle." He remembered his father preaching that horses do not need kudos, treats, and loud affection. They require leadership, safety, and security. This was antithetical to the military mindset of direct action and using force, fear, and intimidation to level the playing field. This was not combat. The horse was not an enemy to neutralize. It was an animal, a broken, scared being needing companionship and cooperation.

The Mustang sensed the sincerity in Jason's approach. It relaxed with a deep exhale, tension falling from its coat like dust. The creature's ears pivoted forward, attuned to the soothing flow of Jason's gently spoken words. This subtle shift marked the deepening of their shallow bond, a connection forged from mutual respect and understanding of each other's intrinsic nature. His father would say, "Horses are herd animals. They thrive with others. If there ain't no others, well, you're it."

Jason's movements were slow and deliberate, echoing the non-predatory behavior his father had so often emphasized. He avoided direct eye contact, giving the Mustang the necessary space to assess him, to understand that he was not a threat, and to let Jason be part of the herd. He remembered his father's analogy, "Be like the gentle breeze that caresses their skin, not the storm that they fear. Be subtle. Make suggestions. Let the horse decide its actions."

Jason spent hours advancing, retreating, and allowing the horse to dictate the situation. "On the horse's terms," his father always said, and Jason was doing just that. The simple task of stepping forward and back, side to side, was a torturous ordeal for Jason. The Yarrow only took the edge off the tremendous pain throbbing through his leg and torso. It was a monumental task. Jason understood what was necessary. He needed to save this horse to rescue himself and ensure their mutual survival.

A soothing embrace held over the land; a whispering breeze caressed the forest's dew-painted leaves. Jason Masters faced the wild Mustang, his heart pounding with the beast's labored breaths. He closed his eyes and took a deep breath, calming himself to connect with the day's tranquility. The barbed wire, a brutal trap set by an indifferent world, ensnared the Mustang, each barb a symbol of the struggles they faced. This moment was an angry volcano, threatening to erupt, to engulf and destroy them both. Jason's hand gripped his Leatherman tool. He moved forward.

As he inched closer, the Mustang's muscles tensed, its eyes wide pools of primal fear. Jason could feel the raw power emanating from the creature, a living force of nature that could erupt into violence at any misstep. Every move he made was calculated—a silent dialogue between man and beast. He remembered his father's teachings—the importance of body language and projecting calmness even if feeling fear. But theory was far different from practice, especially when inches from a frightened, powerful animal.

Jason's first attempt to touch the wire was met with a sudden, defensive jerk from the Mustang. Its hoof struck out, a flash of movement that sent Jason reeling backward, his heart racing. The impact left him winded, a reminder of the precarious line he treads. Blood dripped from a fresh cut on his arm, a result of the Mustang's sudden movement pulling the wire against his skin. Pain shot through him, but it was overshadowed by a more urgent need to help this creature.

With painstaking patience, Jason approached

again, talking in a low, soothing tone. Each word was a drop of hope in an ocean of mistrust. He extended his hand slowly, allowing the Mustang to catch his scent, to see him not as a predator but as an ally. The Leatherman tool dangled from his belt, a necessary evil that promised freedom but also held the risk of disaster.

The minutes stretched into hours as Jason worked to gain the Mustang's trust. Every small step forward was celebrated silently, and every retreat was respected and understood. The dance was delicate, a series of advances and withdrawals, speaking to the intricate language of trust. The Mustang's eyes, once filled with unbridled terror, now flickered with a burgeoning curiosity, a dawning realization that this human might be different.

Finally, after what seemed an age beyond measure, the Mustang granted Jason a restrained permission to approach. The cold, merciless metal of the barbed wire diverged from the living warmth emanating from the creature's heaving sides. With a reverence born of shared pain and understanding, Jason's fingers worked methodically, deftly employing the Leatherman tool to carefully cut and gingerly unwind the wire's hold. Each careful snip resonated like a soft promise of freedom, each gentle tug a deliberate stride toward liberation.

The Mustang's body was a fusion of tension and anticipation. It watched closely with wary suspicion and burgeoning hope. As Jason carefully maneuvered to avoid causing further harm, the animal's flanks quivered, betraying its instinctive urge to flee. Yet, held in place by an emerging trust, it stood still, allowing this human - this unexpected ally - to continue his delicate task. Jason was mindful of checking his reactions, focusing on deep, steady breaths, and his voice was soft and reassuring.

In this toil of liberation, each movement of Jason's hands confirmed his deep understanding of the creature's plight. He moved with an innate knowledge of an unspoken bond with the animal world. The connection transcended verbal language and was communicated through actions of compassion and respect, intent, and energy. The Mustang, in turn, responded to these silent overtures, its rigid posture softening, an unspoken truce forming in the space between retreat and acceptance.

But the task was fraught with danger. The

Mustang, still unpredictable, shifted suddenly, its powerful body moving against the constraints of the wire. Jason felt the sharp sting of the barbs as they sliced into his flesh, a sting that he pushed to the back of his mind. His focus remained unbroken. His resolve was unwavering.

Blood dripped from the laceration in Jason's bicep as the last strand of wire fell away. The Mustang stood free, its body quivering with fear and relief. Bloodied and exhausted, Jason watched as the creature tested its newfound freedom, muscles flexing, hooves stamping the earth tentatively. At that moment, their eyes met, and a silent understanding passed between them. They were no longer just a man and a wild horse; they were survivors, warriors who had faced their fears and emerged stronger.

Jason's heart swelled with an indescribable emotion, a mixture of pride, relief, and a profound respect for the spirit of the Mustang. He had risked everything, his body and soul bare, to save this majestic creature. And in doing so, he had found a piece of himself that he thought was lost in the ravages of war. The Mustang, breathing heavily, its sides heaving with each breath, took a few tentative steps, its movements still cautious but noticeably less constrained. It was a creature reborn, its spirit untethered, yet it lingered as if acknowledging the bond forged in their shared ordeal.

Jason watched, his breaths mirroring the rhythm of the Mustang's. The pain from his wounds was a distant echo compared to the connection he now felt. His hands, bloodied and raw, trembled not just from the exertion but from the emotional weight of the moment. He had stared into the eyes of a wild, untamed force. Instead of chaos, he found understanding and mutual recognition of souls scarred by life's cruelty.

The sun, now higher in the sky, illuminated the rugged beauty of the valley and the two figures within it. Standing together, a human and a horse, Jason bearing the scars of external conflicts and internal struggles, and the Mustang, an emblem of untamed, indomitable liberty.

In the Mustang's wary yet calm demeanor, Jason saw a reflection of his journey, a mirror of his struggle for peace in a world that had often seemed as unforgiving as the barbed wire. He realized that the path to healing was not just about confronting his demons but about embracing the vulnerability and strength that came with facing them.

The Mustang, now free to roam, took a few more steps, its movements more confident. It paused, looking back at Jason with an unspoken gaze of gratitude. Jason nodded a silent farewell, understanding that their paths were meant to cross but not permanently align. The Mustang turned and trotted away, its mane flowing in the wind, a dance of freedom and survival.

As Jason watched the Mustang disappear into the expanse of the valley, he felt a sense of peace settle over him. He had not just freed a Mustang; he had unlocked a part of himself that understood the language of the wild and the unspoken words of the heart. In the wild Mustang, he found a kindred spirit, a guide on his journey toward healing and understanding.

With a deep breath, Jason slowly rose, his wounds aching, but his spirit invigorated. He knew his journey was far from over. Jason also knew he was no longer alone. In the wild heart of the Mustang, he had found a reflection of his own, a reminder that even in the depths of struggle, strength, and beauty are waiting to be discovered.

This encounter was not just about freeing the Mustang from its physical bonds but about liberation. For Jason, it was a journey back to his father's core teachings, a rediscovery of the values that defined horsemanship and relationships. For the Mustang, it was a tentative step toward trusting a member of the species that had often been its oppressor.

As the Mustang faded into the distant horizon, a speck of wild freedom against the sprawling canvas of the San Luis Valley, Jason stood alone, the adrenaline that had fueled his actions rapidly diminishing. The exhilaration of the rescue, the intense focus and energy it had demanded, began to ebb away, leaving him feeling suddenly hollow and drained.

Exhaustion wrapped around him like a heavy cloak, each breath he drew feeling more leaden than the last. Pushed to its limits, his body protested every movement. The cuts from the barbed wire burned. His leg, previously splinted and manageable, now throbbed relentlessly, sending sharp jolts of pain coursing through him with each hobbling step.

The landscape around him seemed vast and

unending. The distance to his vehicle, a mere speck in his memory, loomed impossibly far. He was a solitary figure in the vast wilderness, each step a battle against his own weakening will.

Jason's usually disciplined and resilient mind began to falter under the weight of his physical exhaustion. Dizziness clouded his vision, the world tilting and swaying in a disorienting dance. He fought against the encroaching weakness. His soldier's resolve pushed him to take one more step and then another. But his body was no longer his to command.

Finally, his body made the decision that his mind refused to accept. He stumbled, the earth rushing up to meet him, the tall grasses of the valley softly breaking his fall. As he lay there, the world around him began to dim, the sounds of the wilderness fading into a distant hum. His thoughts drifted to images of wild Mustangs cantering across the grassy plains. He thought of the freedom he had gifted the creature, and in a strange, poetic way, he felt happiness. It was as if by setting the Mustang free, he had also unlocked a part of himself, a part that had been bound by the invisible chains of his past.

As the world faded to black, Jason Masters, the combat veteran, the man who had faced death and despair, found himself surrendering to the uncertain embrace of the valley. His last conscious thought was a whisper, a hope that the Mustang would thrive in its reclaimed freedom. And with that thought, he succumbed to the exhaustion, his body giving in to the much-needed rest, his spirit still tethered to the wild heart of the animal he had saved.

CHAPTER 8

Lessons from the Wild

Jason Masters' eyes fluttered open to the touch of a muzzle against his hand. Startled, his instincts momentarily took him back to hostile territories, but the sight that greeted him was a familiar one— the Mustang. It stood there, a silhouette against the breaking day, its breath a foggy wisp in the cool air.

At that moment, Jason felt a connection, a silent understanding bridging the gap between man and beast. Jason observed a soft, enquiring presence within the Mustang's disposition. It seemed to have recognized Jason as a kindred spirit, a fellow survivor of life's harsh trials, and perhaps even part of the herd. Jason smiled, remembering his father's words, "If there ain't no others, well, you're it."

Jason labored against the sharp jolts of pain that wracked his body. He rose with painstaking slowness, with each movement a deliberate effort to bridge the gap with the Mustang. He extended his hand, trembling slightly under the strain of his injuries, stopping just short of the Mustang's cheek. His heart, thudding against the confines of his bruised chest, found a rhythm in the Mustang's steady breathing—a harmony of trust developing without words. This moment was a poignant dance of two souls intertwined in the language of silent understanding. Each careful gesture from Jason, despite the searing pain, and each contemplative glance from the Mustang added depth to their wordless conversation, an unfolding narrative of empathy and connection. Recalling his father's words, Jason knew the importance of being present and communicating with an authentic presence rather than actions. "Horses speak in the language of the moment," his father used to say. Jason allowed this wisdom to guide him as he approached with respect and curiosity.

Jason was keenly aware of the Mustang's wary

gaze as he slowly moved closer with the adhesive bandages clutched in his aching hands. Each movement he took was cautious, hindered by his discomfort, yet driven by a purpose greater than himself. The Mustang sensed his approach and shifted uneasily, its eyes flickering with curiosity and lingering apprehension.

"Easy, fella," Jason murmured, his voice a soothing balm against the backdrop of the watchful wilderness. He knelt slowly. The Mustang grimaced as his injured leg protested the movement. Muscles tensed, but the horse did not retreat. It was a small but significant sign of emerging trust—an acknowledgment of Jason's intent to heal, not harm.

Cautiously, Jason examined the wounds on the Mustang's legs. The lacerations, though not life-threatening, were raw and needed attention. He remembered the delicate touch his father employed when tending to injured animals back on the farm—a touch that conveyed compassion and understanding. Mimicking that, Jason's hands were steady and gentle despite their bruises and cuts as he cleaned the wounds with a cloth dampened from his water supply.

The Mustang flinched slightly at the first contact, its body tensing, tail harshly swatting the air. Jason paused, allowing the animal time to understand his actions. He spoke in a low, reassuring tone, a habit he'd picked up in the military when trying to calm skittish villagers in distress. Gradually, the Mustang's resistance ebbed, its eyes softening as it began to accept Jason's ministrations.

With great care, Jason applied the adhesive bandages from the fetlocks to the forearms of the front legs. Each wrap acted as a protective shield against the wilderness. The Mustang observed every movement, its ears flicking in response to the unfamiliar sensation of the bandages. It was an intimate, shared experience, each of Jason's careful movements bridging the chasm between human and animal, nurturing their growing bond. Jason moved to the rear legs with trepidation, knowing the power and being aware of the deadlines that a reactive strike could bring. But the wary, ever-present Mustang allowed Jason's healing touch.

Jason sat back on his heels as he finished wrapping the cannon and hocks, observing the Mustang. The creature regarded him with a newfound sense of calm, a silent acknowledgment of the care it had just received. In those eyes, Jason saw an animal he had helped and a reflection of his journey—wounded, resilient, and capable of profound trust.

This act of tending to the Mustang's wounds went beyond physical healing; it was a mutual exchange of faith and understanding. Within Jason's pain and struggle, he found a purpose in caring for a creature that mirrored his plight. And the Mustang, in allowing itself to be cared for, showed a burgeoning trust in the man who offered healing hands. Together, they were navigating a path of mutual healing and companionship, each learning and growing from the other in the silence of the wild.

As hunger gnawed at his insides, Jason's military training surged to the forefront, guiding him through the necessary steps to ensure survival in the rugged Colorado wilderness. He scanned the area, his eyes sharp and focused, searching for edible plants and perhaps even small game, a skill he had honed during his military training in various terrains.

Slowly, he moved towards a patch of wild plants. His knowledge of the local flora, a blend of military survival training, and childhood memories of wandering these lands led him to identify edible berries and roots. He carefully picked wild strawberries and raspberries, their bright reds vibrant among the green foliage. He also unearthed some tubers, resembling small potatoes, knowing he could roast them for a more substantial meal.

Jason returned to his makeshift campsite while the Mustang curiously watched on. Using his Leatherman tool, he struck a flint, and Jason skillfully kindled a small fire. The flames leaped up, casting a warm glow around him. The Mustang, though initially startled by the sudden burst of light and heat, gradually settled down, its gaze fixed on Jason with intrigue.

Jason decided to brew a warm tea. He combined the healing Yarrow leaves with pine needles and sap, creating a medicinal infusion rich in nutrients and antioxidants, a remedy passed down through generations of indigenous peoples to wilderness enthusiasts. The tea's aroma mingled with the pine forest's scent, creating a comforting, earthy fragrance.

As he roasted the tubers and berries on sticks over the fire, Jason reflected on the simplicity and resourcefulness of living off the land. The warmth of the fire, the simple meal, and the company of the Mustang brought a sense of grounding and satisfaction that he hadn't felt since childhood.

The Mustang seemed to sense the calming atmosphere. It edged a bit closer, drawn by the quiet companionship Jason offered. In this shared space, man and beast were together, each a solitary figure in the wilderness, finding a semblance of connection and comfort in each other's presence.

This moment surpassed mere survival. It highlighted Jason's pliability and ability to adapt and thrive in harsh conditions, drawing from the depths of his training and experiences. It was a night where the boundaries between man and nature blurred, where mutual trust and understanding transcended the differences between species, united by the primal instincts of survival and the soothing embrace of the wild.

As the day unfolded the evening, the bond between Jason and the Mustang deepened, evolving beyond coexistence into mutual respect. A wordless bond took root in the serene stillness that enveloped them, echoing the understanding they had achieved. Jason knew he could not navigate out of the mountains with the uneven fields and rocky passes. He glanced at the Mustang, grazing nearby. More than a symbol of freedom, this creature was Jason's freedom. He knew what he needed to attempt. In a moment of ironic humor, Jason heard his father's voice, "Well, what's the worst that can happen?"

The phrase "What's the worst that can happen?" continued to echo in Jason's mind. It was a question that delved deep into the practicalities of his current situation and the philosophical underpinnings of his entire life journey. Each repetition of the question peeled back a layer of anxiety, a layer of unfounded worry, revealing the often-exaggerated nature of fear itself.

As he contemplated the question, Jason realized that the situation could worsen at every response his mind conjured, but to what end? Was it as dire as his mind made it out to be? Even in the most extreme scenario, where death was the outcome, the question challenged him to consider: was that the absolute worst possibility? This relentless inquiry forced Jason to confront the core of his anxieties, questioning the validity of his deepest fears.

This reflective exercise led him down a path of self-realization. It highlighted his worries' absurdity and often unrealistic nature, especially when stacked against the realities of survival in the wilderness. As he pondered, the question began to shift his perspective, offering a more objective and realistic appraisal of his situation.

Jason found himself facing the physical challenges of the wild and confronting the philosophical dimensions of existence and mortality. This simple yet profound question, "What's the worst that can happen?" became a tool for him to dismantle the barriers of fear and anxiety, allowing him to see his circumstances with greater clarity and acceptance.

It was a realization that in the grand scheme of things, most worries were trivial compared to the immediate demands of survival and the ongoing quest for inner peace. As the fire crackled and the Mustang stirred in the background, Jason found a sense of calm and resolve, a newfound understanding that sometimes, facing the worst fears head-on diminishes their power, leaving room for a more balanced and courageous approach to life's challenges. He stood and faced this Mustang.

Reflecting on the wisdom imparted by his father about the subtle nuances of equine behavior, coupled with the patience and observation skills honed in his military training, Jason navigated the space around the Mustang with a respectful awareness. He moved with a composed and deliberate grace, each step and gesture calculated to convey his non-threatening intentions. His movements were slow and measured, mirroring the calm energy he wished to embody, a technique he remembered his father emphasizing as crucial when interacting with horses.

The Mustang seemed to trust Jason. It no longer startled at his approach, instead watching him with a quiet inquisitiveness. The wary distance it had initially maintained started to lessen as if it sensed Jason's deep reverence for its presence. The animal would sometimes approach him, its muzzle tentatively exploring the space around him before retreating to a comfortable distance. This conversation of approach and retreat marked the solidifying trust between them.

Jason continued to reflect on his father's teachings. He remembered how his father would speak of horses as creatures that didn't just listen to words but felt intentions and emotions. "They're mirrors to our souls," his father would say, "reflecting what we put forth." This wisdom guided Jason in his interactions, ensuring his internal state was one of calm and peace despite the pain and hardship he was enduring. "Be a leader. Offer security. Gain its trust. When you can do this, the horse will allow just about anything," his father would preach.

This rhythm of coexistence went beyond mere physical proximity; it was a dance of emotional and spiritual understanding. As Jason tended to his wounds and those of the Mustang, he found his actions becoming more intuitive and more aligned with the needs and comfort of the animal. The Mustang, in turn, began to accept his presence as a reassuring constant in the vastness of the wilderness.

The silent communication between them transcended the boundaries of species. It was a language of empathy, shared experiences of pain and survival, and unspoken understanding and respect. In this quiet communion, man and horse were learning from each other—lessons of patience, trust, and the healing power of companionship.

As the day waned, Jason's thoughts drifted to his military days, to the lessons of resilience and adaptability ingrained in him. He saw parallels in the Mustang's behavior—its cautious approach, its alertness, and its instinctive understanding of the environment. In these reflections, Jason found a newfound appreciation for his past, a realization that every experience, no matter how challenging, had equipped him for moments like these.

Meanwhile, the Mustang seemed to sense Jason's contemplative mood. It inched closer, its nostrils flaring as it caught the scent of the charred wood, the fire's warmth a curious anomaly in its wild existence. Jason watched, a smile tugging at the corners of his mouth, as the Mustang tentatively explored the area around the fire.

That night, as they both settled near the warmth of the dying embers, a silent pact was forged under the starlit sky. Jason, a man who had wandered between worlds, found solace in the company of the Mustang—a creature that mirrored his journey from turmoil to tranquility. For the Mustang, Jason was no longer an intruder in its world but a companion, a fellow traveler on a healing path.

The Mustang's return and willingness to share space with Jason symbolized a new chapter in their journey. It was the power of silent understanding, of bonds formed not through words but through shared experiences and mutual respect.

As Jason lay there, the echoes of his past merging with the present, he realized that this journey was about more than survival. It was about learning and growing, about finding harmony in unexpected places. In the wild heart of the Mustang, he had discovered a reflection of his own—a reminder that even in the most challenging struggles, strength and beauty were waiting to be unearthed.

CHAPTER 9

Bonds of Survival

Jason stirred at the first light of dawn, his body an opus of pain. Each breath was a sharp reminder of his fractured ribs, and his splinted leg lay immobile beside him. The dislocated shoulder, now crudely set back in place, throbbed with every heartbeat. Yet, amid this physical agony, Jason's resolve remained unbroken, fueled by a determination that transcended his injuries.

Lying there, Jason's mind drifted to the many lessons his father had shared, not through written words but through a lifetime of shared experiences and spoken guidance. "In the heart of nature, you find not only your true self but also the truest teachers," his father often said. These teachings, once the background music of his youth, now took center stage, shaping Jason's approach to his current predicament.

Slowly, with a determination that belied his injuries, Jason began the day's work. Each movement was a deliberate act of will, a balance between the physical pain he endured and the mental fortitude he was rediscovering. Though trembling from effort and pain, his hands reached with purpose as he grasped his 550-cord.

Approaching the Mustang, each step was a battle of resilience. His fractured ribs protested with each breath, and his splinted leg was an unwieldy companion, but his resolve was steadfast. Sweat formed on his brow, a mixture of physical exertion and the mental challenge of overcoming his body's limitations.

His father's voice seemed to whisper in the wind, offering unseen support. "Patience is the companion of wisdom," he often reminded Jason during their time together. These words became Jason's anchor as he inched closer to the Mustang, his movements measured and respectful. His father's teachings on patience and empathy now guided his every action, bridging the wisdom of the past and the present challenges.

There was an unspoken understanding between Jason and the Mustang, a mutual acknowledgment of each other's wild and untamed natures. Jason's openness in the face of vulnerability communicated trust to the horse, an unspoken promise that he meant no harm.

With each careful interaction, each gentle brush of the cord against the horse's coat, Jason was doing more than desensitizing the animal; he was forging a bond that transcended mere training. It was a bond built on trust, a silent conversation spoken not in words but in the language of patience and understanding.

As Jason moved, the air around them seemed to hold its breath, the world pausing in reverence to this sacred exchange. The cord, a simple tool, became a bridge between two worlds—human and wild. Each touch of the cord against the Mustang's sleek coat was like a whisper, a promise of safety and companionship.

The Mustang, with its deep, intelligent eyes, watched Jason's every move. There was a quiet wisdom in its gaze, an ancient knowledge that seemed to pierce through the barriers of fear and uncertainty. Each time the cord brushed against its skin, the horse flinched slightly, a natural reaction to the unfamiliar. Yet, the flinching lessened with each pass, replaced by a growing sense of curiosity and acceptance.

Jason's hands, roughened by years of hardship, moved with a surprising tenderness. He understood that each touch was a conversation, each movement a question asked with humility. "Can you trust me?" his actions seemed to inquire. And the horse, with each moment of stillness, each calm breath, replied, "Perhaps, in time."

The Mustang's coat shimmered under the fading sunlight, shades of browns and blacks that seemed to capture the essence of the wild landscape around them. Jason watched as the cord slid over the horse's strong shoulders, along its powerful back, and down its graceful legs. With each pass, a layer of trepidation seemed to fall away, revealing a budding connection, fragile yet resilient.

This was no longer just a man and a horse in the wilderness. It was a meeting of souls. The Mustang's untamed spirit accepted Jason as a partner. And Jason, in turn, saw in the Mustang a reflection of his journey—from isolation to a connection that was as profound as it was unexpected.

In this exchange of trust, a silent dialogue between two beings striving to understand one another, there was a healing power, a sense of peace that seemed to emanate from them, touching the very heart of the wilderness. The world, once a place of solitude and survival, was transforming into a space where two souls could find solace in each other's presence.

As the day progressed, Jason found a rhythm in his movements despite the constant reminder of his injuries. He had crafted a Y-shaped crutch out of fallen branches that took the pressure off his leg. The ache in his shoulder was persistent, yet it was tempered by the horse's growing receptivity to his guidance. This interaction, this dance of mutual respect, offered Jason physical healing and a path to emotional and spiritual recovery.

The late afternoon found Jason and the Mustang in quiet companionship, their shared experiences forming the foundation of an unspoken bond. They were no longer just a wounded man and a wild horse; they had become fellow travelers on a journey of healing and understanding, connected by shared pain, resilience, and a burgeoning sense of trust and mutual respect. It was time.

Jason looked up at the azure Colorado sky, his 550-cord sprawled before him. His fingers, adept and nimble, worked with a sense of purpose ingrained from a childhood spent on his father's farm. As a kid, hundreds of halters had passed through Jason's hands. The wisdom of his father's words echoed in his mind, a guiding force as he meticulously crafted a makeshift halter. His father had once said, "In every strand, there's a lesson of life and patience. Weave them together, not just with skill, but with understanding and respect for the soul you're connecting with."

As he wove the cord, the Mustang stood a short distance away, its coat glistening in the sun, a living embodiment of the wild beauty surrounding them. The halter took shape, each knot a memory of his father's steady hands, each twist a reminder of the silent language spoken between man and horse. With care, Jason braided a lead line from the remaining cord. It was a simple creation, yet it held the weight of countless possibilities.

Approaching the Mustang with the halter in hand, Jason felt a surge of apprehension. This moment was a precipice; the trust they had built could shatter with a single misstep. The air was thick with tension. The only sound was the soft rustling of grass underfoot. He moved with deliberate slowness, each step a gentle plea for understanding.

The Mustang's eyes followed Jason's approach. There was a flicker of uncertainty, a subtle shift in its stance. Jason paused, giving the horse space, his breath a slow, rhythmic cadence syncing with the natural pulse of the wilderness. "The horse will reflect your authentic self, not the mask you portray," Jason remembered his father's teachings, realizing he was tense and unconfident. Horses do not react to predators, per se. They respond to predator behavior. Jason took a breath and recalled: Predators are sneaky, not authentic. They're hiding something. It's OK to be unconfident when around the horse. Just don't pretend not to be. "Be who you are. Be what you are," his father's voice rung in his head.

Jason calmed himself and offered the halter with a patience born of necessity and respect. The Mustang sniffed cautiously, its nostrils flaring. It was a test of mutual vulnerability and the bond they had woven together.

Finally, the halter slid over the Mustang's head, resting gently against its coat. Jason's fingers worked to secure the knot, a silent prayer in each twist. But as the cord cinched, a shadow of fear flashed in the Mustang's eyes. The horse reared in a burst of instinct, a magnificent yet terrifying display of raw power and freedom. Jason stumbled back, falling onto his damaged shoulder with a sharp gasp of pain.

The world narrowed to a point of searing agony. He lay there, a solitary figure against the vast canvas of the valley, controlling his breathing in sharp, deliberate inhales. His eyes clouded with pain but remained fixed on the Mustang. It was now grazing calmly some thirty yards away. Time stretched, each second an eternity, as he watched the embodiment of wild spirit moving with serene grace.

This moment illuminated another profound lesson in horse psychology that Jason recalled from his father's teachings. In the wild, prey animals like horses possess an innate ability to swiftly toggle their fight or flight response. This ability is a survival mechanism embedded in their very essence.

Jason observed the Mustang, its muscles relaxed, its breath steady, as if the burst of fear had been a mere ripple on the surface of a deep lake, now returned to stillness. This rapid return to calm was not a sign of forgetfulness but a necessary adaptation. In the wild, lingering on fear could mean vulnerability to real threats. The Mustang had reacted to the perceived danger of a tightening halter with instinctual fear. But once the threat had passed, it instinctively let go of that fear.

His father's words played in Jason's mind, "Remember, son, a horse lives in the moment. Its survival depends on letting go of fear as quickly as it arises. We must understand this, not fight it." This lesson was more than just an insight into the equine mind; it reflected life itself. Just as the Mustang let go of its fear, Jason realized he must release his past traumas and embrace the present moment.

Watching the Mustang graze peacefully, Jason realized the profound resilience of these magnificent creatures. They did not dwell on past scares or future anxieties. They existed in the now, fully engaged with their environment, yet always ready to respond to real danger. This ability to switch off fear was not just a psychological trait but a profound life skill.

In this understanding, Jason found a mirror to his own journey. Like the Mustang, he, too, had been gripped by a fight or flight response, haunted by shadows of his past. But now, as he watched this wild creature, a realization dawned upon him. The key to healing and moving forward was not holding onto fear but learning to let it go and to exist in the present. Just as the Mustang did with such graceful resilience.

Jason found a powerful metaphor for his life in the Mustang's simple act of grazing after a moment of intensity. It was a lesson in survival, resilience, and the transformative power of understanding and embracing the natural wisdom of letting go.

The memory came to Jason as he watched the Mustang—a vignette from his childhood, vivid and enduring. He was standing in the dusty paddock of his father's farm. They were with an indifferent horse, a beautiful but aloof mare that seemed more interested in the distant mountains than the humans trying to reach her.

His father, a man of few words but deep under-standing, turned to Jason and said, "You have to make yourself interesting, son. Capture their attention somehow. Be something, someone that makes them curious." There was a twinkle in his eye, a hint of a shared secret, as he turned his attention back to the horse.

Jason watched, fascinated, as his father began to employ a technique that seemed counterintuitive. Instead of approaching the mare directly, he walked around her in arcs and spaghetti-like trajectories. It was a dance of avoidance, a deliberate act of ignoring that seemed to go against everything a young, eager Jason believed about getting a horse's attention.

His father's eyes were focused elsewhere, deliberately looking away from the mare, his attention seemingly captured by something mundane in the paddock. It was just a tiny rock, but to his father, it was a tool, an actor in this silent play of curiosity. He bent down and picked up the rock, turning it over in his hands and examining it as if it held the secrets of the universe. He brushed the sand and dirt away from it, dropped it, and then picked it up again, moving it around in a show of quiet fascination.

This simple act, so out of place in the context

of horse training, was a stroke of subtle genius. The mare, initially indifferent, couldn't help but be drawn in by this unusual behavior. Her ears twitched, and her eyes followed his father's movements. Slowly, almost imperceptibly at first, she began to move toward him. It was as if an invisible rope of curiosity was pulling her closer.

Jason's father continued his act, never once making direct eye contact with the mare, never acknowledging her approach. It was as if the rock in his hand was the most exciting thing in the world. And to the mare, this became a mystery she felt compelled to solve.

Finally, after what seemed like an eternity to young Jason, the mare was close enough to sniff his father's hand, which still held the rock. At that moment, his father gently turned, offering the mare the back of his hand to smell. There was no sudden movement, no rush of emotion, just a quiet, patient acknowledgment of her presence.

The mare sniffed his hand, her body language shifting from indifference to interest. At that moment, a connection was made, a bridge built not through force or intimidation but through the power of curiosity and gentle intrigue.

Watching from the sidelines, Jason realized that his father had imparted a lesson far greater than horse training. It was a lesson about life, how patience, indirect approaches, and making oneself interesting could open doors and build connections that seemed initially unreachable. This memory, etched in the fabric of his being, became a guiding light in his journey with the wild Mustang, a journey of understanding, patience, and the subtle art of winning trust.

As the memory of his father's wisdom faded, Jason turned his attention to the present. He rose from the ground, his shoulder aching with a dull, persistent throb. The Mustang was still yards away, watching him with an air of nonchalant curiosity, its deep, dark eyes following his every movement.

Jason began to pack up his camp, deliberately focusing on the task at hand. He folded his bivy with precise, methodical movements, each fold a meditation. As he stowed it away, the clinking of camping gear seemed to punctuate the silent wilderness around him. Jason was acutely aware of the Mustang's gaze but did not acknowledge it. Instead, he immersed himself in the mundanity of his chores, creating an aura of apathy.

The Mustang, intrigued by this man who had suddenly become an enigma, continued to graze with an evident mindfulness of Jason's presence. It was a subtle game of silent watching and waiting. The horse's ears twitched occasionally in Jason's direction, betraying its growing interest.

Once everything was packed and his campsite was restored to its natural state, Jason slung his backpack over his good shoulder. Without a backward glance at the Mustang, he started walking in the opposite direction. His steps were forced and pain-trodden, but he kept a steady, deliberate cadence that spoke of purpose and resolve. Jason did not look back, not even once.

Minutes passed, each one stretching longer than the last. Then, the sound of soft hoofbeats broke the silence. The Mustang, compelled by curiosity, made subtle movements toward Jason. At first, it was a hesitant step, then another, until it broke into a gentle trot, quickly closing the distance between them.

Jason, maintaining his role in this silent play, continued to ignore the presence of the horse. His heartbeat was a mix of anticipation and calm, mirroring the inner transformation he was under-going.

The Mustang caught up to him, now walking at his side. It was a quiet, powerful display of companionship, a choice made not out of necessity but of connection. The horse then began to nuzzle Jason's shoulder with its nose, an affectionate gesture that spoke louder than any words. It gave him a quick, playful nip, signifying its growing comfort and trust.

Then, with a nonchalance born of deep understanding, Jason gently gripped the braided lead line. The action was a subtle physical manifestation of the invisible bond steadily forming between them.

They moved, man and horse, united by a shared journey. The wilderness around them seemed to acknowledge this union, the late afternoon sun casting a warm, golden light that enveloped them in an ethereal glow.

As they moved in harmony, Jason felt enveloped in peace. The horse allowed a firm grip on the lead, helping Jason navigate and keeping some weight off the injured leg. The pain in Jason's shoulder seemed to dull, overshadowed by this unlikely connection he now shared with the Mustang. They were no longer just a man and a wild horse; they were companions, each a vital part of the other's story—of each other's survival.

Do or Die

Jason Masters and the wild Mustang embarked on a perilous journey back to civilization. As they traversed the rugged terrain, the bond between man and horse was continually tested against the backdrop of nature's harsh beauty.

Jason Masters found himself in a dire predicament. His leg, marred by a festering infection, throbbed with searing pain, transforming each step into a laborious endeavor. The once crisp, invigorating mountain air now felt heavy, laden with the weight of his struggle. Around him, the untamed forest witnessed his plight; its dense underbrush and uneven terrain were unyielding obstacles to his progress.

In a moment of desperation tinged with ingenuity, Jason's gaze fell upon the scattered branches around him. They were remnants of the wild, twisted and sturdy, shaped by the unforgiving elements of nature. With hands quivering from pain and determination, he carefully selected the most robust limbs, their bark rough under his touch. These branches, he surmised, could be his salvation. Painstakingly, he fashioned a makeshift handhold, a rudimentary yet vital tool born from the heart of the wilderness. It was a crude construction, but in his hands, it was a lifeline and a means to persevere.

The Mustang observed intently. Its dark eyes flickered a spark of understanding, a silent acknowledgment of the bond they had formed. This was not the distant, wary gaze of a wild animal. It was a look of comprehension, born from the time they weathered together. The Mustang had been a solitary wanderer of the vast Colorado expanse. Nonetheless, it found an unspoken kinship in Jason's presence.

Sensing Jason's struggle, the Mustang shifted

its stance, its muscles rippling under its glossy coat. In a gesture of remarkable trust, it allowed Jason to lean against its sturdy frame, using it as a balance point. This was no small feat for a creature that epitomized the essence of the wild. The Mustang seemed to recognize the gravity of their situation. It stood steady and patient, breathing calmly and rhythmically, providing Jason with desperately needed support.

With the handhold in one hand and his other hand resting gently on the Mustang's flank, Jason began to navigate the challenging terrain. Each step was a concerted effort between man and beast. The Mustang moved with deliberate steps, mindful of Jason's limitations, adjusting its pace to accommodate his unsteady gait. It was a walk of survival as they advanced with a purpose that transcended instincts.

Together, they traversed rocky inclines, their path illuminated by the soft, golden light filtering through the dense canopy above. Streams, once mere trickles in the landscape, now posed significant hurdles. The Mustang navigated them with a grace that belied its size. Jason, leaning heavily on his makeshift handhold, matched his movements to the rhythm of the Mustang's strides. Their connection deepened, transcending the boundaries between man and wild creature.

The journey was arduous, but within it lay a transformation. Jason, guided by the Mustang's unwavering strength, found a reservoir of resilience within himself. Each step forward was a triumph over the adversity they faced, a step closer to the salvation that lay beyond the wilderness. In this journey, marked by shared struggles and mutual dependence, Jason and the Mustang forged an unbreakable bond, a union of spirits that would endure long after their journey had ended.

Jason and the Mustang arrived at a river, its waters cascading with a ferocity that mirrored Jason's tumultuous heart. The river was a ribbon of churning, icy blue, cutting through the landscape with unrelenting force. Its fast-moving currents spoke of the untamed spirit of nature, both beautiful and intimidating in its power.

With a natural grace, the Mustang approached the riverbank, lowering its head to drink from the cool waters. Jason watched the creature, finding peace in the simple act. Yet, as he observed the water's relentless flow, a knot of apprehension tightened in his chest. The crossing would be precarious—a formidable challenge for his injured state.

After allowing themselves a momentary respite, Jason steeled himself for the crossing. He took a deep breath, the cool, moist air filling his lungs as if drawing strength from the very essence of the wilderness around him. Man and horse stepped cautiously into the river, the icy water swirling around their legs.

Hidden beneath the deceptive clarity of the water was a treacherous labyrinth of stones and pebbles. Each step was a gamble, the unstable rocks shifting treacherously underfoot. The Mustang navigated the path with an innate sure-footedness, but for Jason, every movement was a struggle against the relentless pull of the current.

As they waded deeper, the water's pace quickened, its force amplified. The river showed no mercy for the weary travelers. Jason leaned heavily on his makeshift handhold, fighting to maintain his balance. But the river seemed to conspire against him. His broken, infected leg, already a source of excruciating pain, could no longer bear the strain. With a heart-wrenching twist, he fell, his leg buckling beneath him, the bone dislocating with a jolt of pain that radiated through his entire body.

Instantly, Jason vanished beneath the river's tumultuous surface. Paralyzed by agony, the relentless current sought to claim him, pulling him under the Mustang's powerful form. In a desperate, almost instinctive effort, Jason gutted out his hand, grasping. His grip found its mark on the Mustang's pastern. Sensing the urgency, the horse countered the river's force, firmly anchoring its legs against the shifting riverbed. Steadfast, it stood as Jason clambered up its leg to secure the looped 550-cord around the Mustang's neck. The Mustang began its determined trek toward the shore. Jason clung on, his body buffeted by the unyielding waters, each effort a battle against nature's overwhelming strength.

As they reached the riverbank, the Mustang meandered to a nearby area of inviting green grass. Jason lay on the shore, gasping for breath. The pain in his leg was overwhelming. He peered toward the Mustang with gratitude in his heart. The Mustang had become Jason's savior, his ally in adversity. Jason watched as the Mustang continued to graze. He changed his gaze to his leg, knowing it needed immediate attention.

Jason found himself facing a grim reality. His lower leg, a crucial pillar of his strength, was now a source of intense agony. The fibula was unmistakably broken, its alignment skewed in a way that made Jason's stomach churned. The tibula was most likely fractured. It was a painful but less severe injury. As the realization set in, Jason understood what he had to do. The thought of resetting his fibula bone was daunting. The alternative, however, was to remain immobile, a prisoner of his injuries. This was not an option.

Drawing a deep breath, Jason surveyed his surroundings. The untamed wilderness now served as his makeshift operating room. He gathered what he could from the environment: sturdy branches, strong enough to serve as supports; strips of bark and smaller twigs for additional reinforcement; and the remnants of his clothing to use as binding.

Jason Masters, grappling with his broken lower leg, faced a daunting task. His emotions teetered between determination and apprehension. Every fiber of his being braced for what he knew would be an agonizing process.

With a deep, steadying breath, Jason prepared to reset his leg. Tying one end of his 550-cord around his ankle and looping the other around a nearby tree, he created a makeshift pulley. His hands, though shaking, were driven by the sheer will to survive. As he pulled the cord, exerting gentle traction, the pain surged like wildfire through his leg, drawing a guttural cry from his lips. The pain was almost blinding, but Jason's resolve did not waver.

Once the bone slipped back into place, a momentary relief washed over him, swiftly replaced by throbbing pain. He quickly fashioned a splint from branches and clothing, wrapping it snugly yet cautiously around his leg to immobilize it. Each movement, each tightening of the cord, was a battle against both pain and the fear of what lay ahead.

As Jason lay back against the earth, his breaths ragged with exertion and pain, he realized the gravity of his situation. The rigid and confining splint would make the journey ahead more challenging. Despite the pain and the daunting path ahead, he knew he had to mount the Mustang and ride for help. Jason prepared for the impossible task ahead.

Jason's thoughts drifted to his father's wisdom as he rested on the soft earth. The teachings of natural horsemanship and his childhood memories of his father training and riding horses became a beacon of hope in the enveloping darkness. Drawing strength from these recollections, Jason knew it was time to deepen their connection. He mustered all his knowledge and willpower to work with the Mustang. With painstaking agony, he rose and faced the horse.

Jason faced the formidable challenge with an Achillean determination. This task would be daunting under normal circumstances. It would now test his resilience and his bond with the Mustang. He would need to remember and rely on the natural horsemanship techniques passed down by his father.

Burdened by his splinted leg and rejecting his physical pain, Jason approached the Mustang. The sun glowed warmly on the scene, highlighting the subtle nuances of their interaction. Jason's initial touch on the Mustang's back was a tender overture, his hands conveying a message of trust and reassurance. The Mustang stood fast, already accustomed to the weight of Jason's handhold. Jason continued applying increasing pressure, followed by a gentle release each time the Mustang started to tense. It was like a whispered conversation, a language of comfort and safety that resonated with the horse.

As their mutual confidence grew, so did the weight of the applied pressure. With deep respect and care, Jason smoothly draped his arms over the horse's back. This was a physical act and an emblem of trust and security. The Mustang responded with a composure that spoke volumes. With steady breaths, it stood unwavering, accepting the increasing weight with an ease that hinted at understanding. Seemingly unphased, it continued to graze.

The rhythm of Jason's movements, the push and release of his arms, mirrored the natural cadence of the world around them. It was a dialogue of trust, a harmonious interplay between man and horse. The Mustang's eyes reflected curiosity and awareness. It followed Jason's every move, its body language an open book to his intentions.

Nestled in the heart of the wilderness, Jason savored the unspoken bond between them. It was a display of mutual respect, a shared journey that transcended the barriers between the wild and the tamed. As this new level of partnership was forged, Jason could not help but admire this Mustang's curiosity and willingness. Or was it something else?

As the sun arched toward the Western sky, Jason knew he needed to accelerate the process. The Mustang continued to display tranquility and understanding that hinted at past interaction with humans, suggesting it was not as wild as Jason believed. He stood beside the Mustang, drawing from his generational wisdom. "Trust is earned, not given," his father's words echoed in his mind, a mantra that guided his every action.

Jason began the meticulous process of familiarizing the Mustang with this process. With agonizing effort, he would hop up and down slightly, the motion akin to mounting. He was mindful of the horse's body language, careful not to startle it. At first, the Mustang responded with a skittish shuffle, its muscles tensing, eyes wide with caution. Jason, acknowledging this reaction, would cease his movement, releasing the pressure and offering the horse a moment of calm. It also provided Jason a minute reprieve from the pain radiating through his ribcage and lower leg.

As Jason continued, he remembered another

of his father's teachings: "In their eyes, you'll find their heart." Watching the Mustang's eyes, he could sense its apprehension and waited patiently for it to subside.

Gradually, the Mustang's body language softened, and it willingly accepted the rhythm of Jason's movements. It became inquisitive while it learned this game. The horse's ears were relaxed and occasionally twitched forward, tuning into Jason's movements. With each effortful hop, Jason observed the Mustang's reaction, ensuring that he maintained a space of respect and understanding.

Jason carefully increased the vigor of his movements. He would hop a little higher, his hand putting pressure on the Mustang's back. Now more accustomed to his actions, the Mustang stood with a steadier demeanor. Its gaze followed Jason's ascent and descent. "Horses love to play," Jason's father would say, "Make it a game, and you will capture their attention and willingness to engage." Jason smiled as the Mustang bobbed its head and swished its tail in playful gestures.

Feeling the connection and trust established, Jason prepared to drape his body over the Mustang's back. He led the Mustang to a downed tree trunk that offered elevation for the task. He positioned himself on the trunk alongside the horse. Jason reassessed the creature's willingness by reestablishing connected hand pressure on its back. The Mustang stood with one rear leg slightly bent in relaxation. Jason hopped slightly for a few more moments, putting pressure on the horse's back. The horse seemed indifferent, nibbling on the green grass next to the tree trunk.

Jason took a deep breath to steady his nerves and ease the pain in his body. With a gentle but firm touch, he placed his hands on the Mustang's back. Gathering his strength, Jason attempted to lift himself, aiming to lie across the Mustang's back. It was a significant step that required the Mustang's acceptance and willingness. As he lifted himself, the Mustang shifted slightly, a natural reaction to the unfamiliar weight. Jason paused and held his position, allowing the horse to adjust to his weight. The air was thick with anticipation, a quiet understanding passing between man and beast.

At that moment, the teachings of his father and the principles of natural horsemanship merged into a singular focus. It was not just about the physical act of mounting but about creating a bond of mutual respect and understanding, a partnership forged through patience and empathy. Jason was ready to fully commit, to trust in the bond he had formed with the Mustang, and to attempt to swing his body over its back.

Carefully, Jason lowered himself over the Mustang's back. The Mustang stood unaffected, continuing to graze. Jason felt an understanding from the Mustang that suggested familiarity with this action, an awareness beyond wild instincts.

Slumped over the Mustang, Jason paused to deepen their connection, gently stroking its mane. This dead man's position allowed his leg to be free of unwanted weight, reducing pain levels significantly. However, Jason's ribs were another story. His injured torso was now holding his weight on the Mustang's back. Jason struggled to breathe. But there was no urgency for movement, no immediate action needed, so he relaxed into the pain, releasing all the tension from his body. The Mustang continued to be unaffected, taking small steps munching on grass.

Jason recognized the significance of this moment. As he lay draped across the Mustang's back, he fully embraced the experience. With Jason's complete surrender, the Mustang took the initiative, moving at its own pace while Jason collapsed on its back. There was an air of mutual respect and trust, a culmination of their shared experiences and the principles of natural horsemanship that Jason had so carefully applied. In this quiet triumph, their partnership was solidified, a relationship born of necessity, mutual understanding, and respect. Amidst the untamed wilderness, man and horse ventured forward.

CHAPTER 11

Healing in Nature

The Colorado wilderness stretched endlessly around Jason and the Mustang. Jason lay slumped over the Mustang, a posture that spoke volumes about their shared plight. Their injuries, both visible and hidden, worsened with each passing mile, sapping their strength and diminishing hopes of survival.

As the Mustang steadily moved through the dense underbrush, Jason's consciousness drifted into a realm where the present and past collided. The physical agony of his injuries and the weariness of the journey drew him into a semi-conscious state. In this space, memories from his military service resurfaced with haunting clarity. These recollections, emerging from his mind, were as vivid and jarring as the wilderness he now found himself in.

As Jason's mind slipped into the chasm of his past, he was transported back to a scene etched in his most harrowing memories. It was a village ravaged by the relentless scourge of war. The air was thick with dust and the acrid smell of smoke. The tension was tangible; it seemed to cling to his skin. The once vibrant streets were now in ruin and despair, a haunting echo of a long-gone time.

The weight of his rifle was so familiar, an extension of his arm, a harbinger of both protection and destruction. His heart pounded, a drumbeat in sync with the quickening pace of impending conflict. Jason held overwatch. His eyes continually scanned for threats. They were the only part of him that moved, darting from shadow to shadow in a maze of devastation.

Then, chaos erupted. A fury of bullets and shouts, the sounds sharp jabs to his senses, as his team engaged the enemy. The 82nd's reaction was fierce and intense. Jason identified multiple targets in windows, behind blown-out vehicles, and hinging on corners of buildings. His instincts were sharp as he quickly neutralized several targets.

In the madness, a figure emerged, darting with desperate speed from behind the skeletal remains of a wall. Instinct took over, honed by countless hours of training and the primal urge to survive. Jason's finger pressured the trigger, an action as reflexive as breathing. The rifle recoiled against his shoulder, a violent confirmation of his deadly response.

Time seemed to slow in the aftermath, the cacophony around him fading into a distant hum. As the dust swirled and settled like a shroud over the scene, the brutal reality of his action became heartbreakingly clear. The figure that lay motionless on the ground was no seasoned soldier, no hardened warrior. It was a child, barely a teenager, his life extinguished in the blink of an eye. An AK-47 lay discarded near the small, lifeless hand.

Jason stood frozen, the rifle in his hands now feeling like a leaden weight of guilt. The child's face, frozen in surprise and fear, was seared into Jason's memory, an indelible image that would haunt his dreams and waking moments. The innocence lost, the future stolen, all in the name of a conflict that chewed up lives and spat out only sorrow and regret.

That irreversible heartbeat of a decision became a ghost that followed Jason, a constant whisper of what was lost. It illuminated the fine line between duty and humanity. The ruthless nature of war often claimed youth and innocence as casualties in the fight for survival.

Tears breached the corners of Jason's eyes as his mind took him to a different scene. On a critical mission, his team had hitched a ride with an infantry convoy.

Suddenly, IEDs and mortar rounds exploded, lighting vehicles ablaze as screams pierced the air. As the squad leader, Jason had made a call to move out, leaving behind the wounded, a decision dictated by critical mission protocol but against his moral compass. The guilt of leaving comrades and the crushing weight of leadership in times of crisis left deep scars in his psyche.

These memories were not just recollections of events; they were reflections of deep internal conflict within his mind, as his combat actions often contradicted his core values. Jason had always believed in honor, in protecting the innocent, and in the sanctity of life. Yet, the brutal necessities of war forced him to act against these beliefs, leaving him with an unshakable sense of guilt and betrayal.

In the present, as the Mustang navigated the rugged terrain, Jason grappled with these feelings. The Mustang, in its way, seemed to sense this inner turmoil. It responded to his shifting emotions with subtle, intuitive gestures—a gentle nudge, a soft nicker—offering comfort and a semblance of understanding.

Jason found solace in speaking to the Mustang as if it were an old comrade who could comprehend his heartache. He shared stories of his fallen friends, the moments of fear and courage, and the bond he shared with his unit. The Mustang became a silent confidante, its presence a balm to his wounded soul.

Jason realized the Mustang's presence was helping him confront his deepest fears and regrets. It was as if the horse, with its history of wildness and struggle, understood the complexity of his emotions. This realization brought a new perspective to his relationship with the Mustang, transforming it from a mere companion to a partner in his journey of healing and self-discovery.

The deluge of Jason's memories was relentless, each one a piercing shard of his past, unraveling him from within. Tears silently streamed down his face as these recollections surged through his mind. Each drop was an inner torment—a blend of sorrow, regret, and unspoken apologies. Jason was acutely aware of his precarious situation, each step either a progression toward salvation or a descent into the inescapable embrace of death. The journey was a tightrope walk over an abyss, where every falter could mean the end.

Yet, paradoxically, as he waded through this sea of painful memories, a sense of unburdening began to take hold. It was as if each tear that fell was a carrier of his pain, guilt, and shame, washing away fragments of the burden he had carried for so long. This emotional catharsis, though heart-wrenching, was liberating. He felt the weight of his past gradually lifting, leaving behind a solemn resolve. Deep in his heart, he knew that survival was not just about making it out alive but about emerging as a transformed individual. If fate granted him the chance to continue his journey beyond this wilderness, he vowed to be better for himself and the world around him. He would strive to become a better person, a better human being, shaped by the lessons learned and the compassion found in the depths of his despair.

A surge of determination ignited within Jason, burning like a beacon in the darkness of pain and exhaustion. Every fiber of his being screamed in protest as he summoned an inner strength he barely recognized. Gritting his teeth against the aching that ravaged his body, he began the grueling task of lifting himself from the slumped position that had become his refuge in weakness.

With a deep, labored breath, Jason braced his arms. He felt the coarse texture of the Mustang's mane beneath his palms. Sensing the shifting weight, the Mustang braced, its muscles tense yet supportive. Although wracked with throbbing pain, Jason's good leg became the pillar of his strength as he swung it over the Mustang's back. It was a slow, painstaking maneuver, an epic challenge of his endurance.

A transformation unfolded within him as he sat upright, straddling the Mustang's powerful back. This was no mere physical readjustment; it symbolized his inner grit and tenacity. Jason was no longer a man defined by his injuries and haunted by his past; he was a warrior rising from the ashes of his despair.

Sitting tall on the Mustang, Jason felt a rush of wind against his face, a sensation that breathed life into his weary soul. His heart raced in a rhythm that spoke of life, of survival. The act of sitting upright, facing forward, was a declaration to the world and himself. He was not merely enduring; he was prevailing.

In this upright posture, Jason embodied a newfound courage, a readiness to confront whatever lay ahead. The path forward was uncertain, but he was resolute in facing it head-on. This was more than a journey through the wilderness; it was a journey toward healing, toward redemption, and a future he was now determined to forge with courage and resolve.

There was still a long way to go. Although his mind had gained renewed strength, his body continued to weaken. He noticed the Mustang's gait was slower, its breath labored, and it frequently stumbled—telltale signs of a fading strength. As night began to envelop the landscape, Jason and the Mustang, both drained by their ordeal, skirted the mountain's edge, making their way out. In the distance, a flicker of light pierced the encroaching darkness. It could be a house, a campfire, perhaps a beacon of salvation.

CHAPTER 12

A New Understanding

Under the vast, star-studded sky, Jason Masters and the wild Mustang trudged on. The movement was slow, with each of the Mustang's steps heavily labored with deep huffs of effort. Both weary and wounded, they advanced toward the distant flicker of light. It was an elusive beacon in the dark forest that seemed impossibly far.

As they moved, the quiet of the night was broken only by the soft crunch of the Mustang's deep breathing and footfalls. Jason constantly tried to stay upright, his body protesting, pulling him downward. His thoughts wandered back to his childhood, to the days spent watching his father work with horses. Those memories, once buried under the debris of war and pain, now resurfaced with clarity and insight.

His father always said, "Understanding a horse is like understanding a river; you must watch it flow, learn its course, and respect its power." Memories of his father's words echoed in his mind, not just as distant whispers of the past but as living wisdom guiding his present.

Jason realized that his father's horsemanship wisdom was also about life itself. The principles of natural horsemanship—pressure and release, approach and retreat, reward and consequences—were metaphors for human relationships and personal growth.

His father had imparted wisdom with a gentle yet profound understanding, emphasizing that it was more than just a training technique; it was a vital aspect of communication and connection. "Remember, son," his father would say with a knowing look, "pressure and release aren't about exerting dominance. It's a dialogue, a language without words. It's about understanding and feeling the horse, knowing when to ask more and when to ease off. Just like the push and pull of the ocean tides, it's about balance and harmony."

This ethos of natural horsemanship had become a metaphor for Jason. In his interactions with the wild Mustang, he saw a reflection of his struggles and triumphs. Applying pressure was like confronting his fears and challenges head-on, not to overpower them but to acknowledge their presence. The release was akin to the moments of letting go, of understanding that some battles were won not through force but through understanding and patience. Jason had always approached situations and people with a certain amount of force and direct action. He realized that his intimidating manner would not work for him in the civilian world.

Jason began to see parallels between the horse's responses and his own internal battles. The Mustang's initial resistance mirrored Jason's propensity to face situations with force and his habit of hiding fear and pain behind an ersatz mask. Yet, as Jason surrendered to his authenticity, the horse gradually trusted and responded.

"In the rhythm of pressure and release lies the dance of understanding and empathy," his father had said. It was a lesson that transcended the realm of horse training, touching the core of human experience and interaction. Jason realized that this was not about his relationship with the Mustang. It represented his journey toward healing and finding a new rhythm in life. A rhythm that embraced acceptance and the beauty of recovery.

"You must be aware of your presence and mindful of the pressure you exert," lectured his father. Jason's father taught him that every person had a different essence and exerted varying levels of pressure on the world. Some people are unknowingly powerful, while others are delicate. Strong people must learn finesse, while the more delicate must learn assertiveness. His father would say, "It's all about balance in the moment. Using the right amount of pressure with the appropriate release. But remember, every moment is different."

Jason finally understood the wisdom in his father's teachings. Time is continually transitional, and each moment needs to be reassessed and balanced. He had always faced each tick of the second hand with the same power and force as the last, never noticing subtle changes in people or the environment. This had served its purpose and worked well for him in the military as a leader and in combat situations. Still, Jason now saw the barriers and struggles it created.

Jason continued to reflect on how his father's wisdom juxtaposed with his ever-intimidating character. Jason remembered his father had taught him about pressure and release and how to physically *be* in the presence of horses. In the corridors of his memories, his father's voice resonated, "Approach and retreat is much more than a mere technique. It's an art. Like carefully choreographed steps, you draw near and then give space. It's about creating a rhythm of trust and respect. It's not merely about training the horse but inviting it into a partnership."

In the technique of approach and retreat, Jason saw more than the physical movements; he saw a metaphor for life and societal existence. He recognized that in every step he took toward the Mustang, he also stepped closer to the fragmented pieces of his spirit. Each retreat was not a defeat but a necessary respite, a moment to gather strength. Jason realized these lessons bode well in a world of diversity and varying personalities. He acknowledged he couldn't just always leap forward with the ferocity of his character. There needs to be a delicate exchange of energy that allows for mutual respect, security, and communication between each person.

Approach and retreat is a delicate balance between respecting boundaries and breaking down walls. It was about knowing when to push forward and when to step back, not just with the Mustang but within himself and with the world.

Jason's father would say, "Approach and retreat is a symphony of patience, trust, and mutual respect. It's not just about training a horse; it's learning to tame your soul's chaos, to approach your deep fears, and retreat only to return stronger and more resilient." Jason realized this experience taught him more about himself than he had ever known.

The rigid military command structure lingered in Jason's mind like an old, unyielding tree, its roots entwined with his thoughts and actions. In that world, orders cascaded down a steep hierarchy, leaving no room for debate or dissent. It was a world where commands were uttered, and obedience was the only acceptable response. While effective in the field, this strict adherence to order and discipline often left little space for personal reflection or emotional growth. It was a world far removed from the nuanced complexities of civilian life, the fluid, dynamic interactions that define our societal and cultural experiences.

This structure was etched deeply into Jason's psyche and cast a long shadow over his attempts to reintegrate into a world that thrived on dialogue and cooperation rather than unilateral commands. The military's black-and-white view of obedience and consequence had, in many ways, ill-prepared him for the gray areas of civilian life, where empathy, understanding, and collaboration are the cornerstones of relationships and personal development.

As Jason pondered the distinct approaches to leadership and guidance, his thoughts naturally drifted to the art of horsemanship, particularly the gentle, compassionate methods his father had championed. His father's teachings contrasted greatly with the military's rigid structure. "Reward and consequences," his father had often said, with a voice as calm as a quiet stream, "are not about wielding power but about understanding the soul. It's not about demanding respect through fear but earning it through empathy. We are not looking for compliance. We are inviting partnership and collaboration."

His father's dialogue whorled in Jason's head, weaving through his memories like a soothing melody. He recalled how his father would work with the horses, his movements deliberate but gentle, always mindful of the horse's response. He moved with respect, where each step was about understanding and trust, not dominance. This approach was about nurturing a bond that was built on the foundation of mutual regard and understanding.

This philosophy of natural horsemanship, rooted in empathy and cooperation, resonated with Jason's journey toward self-compassion. He began to see his path to healing not as a series of commands to be followed but as opportunities for growth and self-discovery. Each small step forward was a victory to be savored. The consequences of his actions, he realized, were not punishments meted out by a strict commander. These lessons shaped his journey, guiding him toward a deeper understanding of himself and the world around him.

In this new light, Jason began to embrace his

experiences in the military and the wilderness of Colorado as integral parts of his journey. Each experience, whether a command followed, a fall from a mountain, or a gentle interaction with a horse, was a thread in the fabric of his life, weaving together a story of transformation and renewal.

These principles of natural horsemanship were life lessons his father had imparted. They were lessons about respect, communication, trust, patience, and understanding. As Jason gazed into the Mustang's eyes, he felt a profound connection, not just with the creature before him but with the wisdom that transcended the divide between man and horse. At that moment, he understood that his path to healing and wholeness was mirrored in the wild spirit of the Mustang, in the unspoken bond they formed, a bond fostered through adversity and the timeless wisdom of his father's teachings.

In the Mustang, Jason found a connection he had lost with people. The horse's reactions were honest, its emotions unguarded. Unlike humans, it did not judge or pity; it simply existed in the moment. This purity, this absence of pretense, was what Jason had missed in human interactions, where words were often barriers rather than bridges.

The journey through the night became a journey through his past. Memories of his mother's gentle touch and his father's wise words intermingled with the harsh realities of combat and the alienation of returning home. He recalled his father's words, "Trust is earned, son, both in the saddle and in life. It's a give and take." Jason understood now that his reintegration into civilian life required the same patience and understanding he practiced with the Mustang.

In the Mustang's resilience, Jason saw his own. The wild, wounded horse had learned to accept his presence, not as a captor, but as a companion. Similarly, Jason realized that he could embrace his past without being imprisoned by it. He could blend the strength and vigilance of the soldier with the empathy and vulnerability of the man he wanted to become.

As the first light of dawn filtered through the trees, Jason and the Mustang arrived at the source of light. It was a quaint ranch, the distant cabin, humble and welcoming. It was accompanied by a sturdy barn, a vast field, and a large paddock where several horses grazed peacefully.

The Mustang's coat was matted, and its breaths came in shallow heaves. It moved with a forced resilience that mirrored Jason's own. Jason was slumped forward, his hands gripping the Mustang's mane. He was the embodiment of exhaustion. Heavy with fatigue, his eyes struggled to stay open, yet there was a determined glint, an unfaltering will to survive and overcome.

As they neared the field's boundaries, a gate came into view. Jason mustered his last reserves of strength and reached to unlatch it. The sound of the gate creaking open seemed to echo in the silence of the dawn. Just then, a figure appeared in the distant barn doorway, a shadow against the lightening sky. The sudden bark of a dog pierced the morning air, startling both Jason and the Mustang.

As the Mustang cautiously entered the field, Jason's hold relaxed. His exhausted body could no longer resist the overwhelming fatigue. He slipped from the horse's back, collapsing to the ground as the world around him dimmed into silence. Their arduous journey had exacted its price. The dawn sky, adorned with soft golden-orange streaks, stretched above Jason Masters, who now lay motionless at the paddock's edge. He surrendered to unconsciousness.

CHAPTER 13

Rescued

In the cool, tranquil light of the early dawn, Sydney Blake moved with a grace that belied the toughness of her daily labor. Her hands, calloused and strong, worked skillfully as she mucked the stalls and tended to the equine residents of her farm - a mix of horses and donkeys, each with their unique personality and story.

The farm, nestled in the heart of the Colorado wilderness, was more than just a piece of land to Sydney. It was a sanctuary where her soul found peace and her heart a sense of purpose. With its undulating fields and towering pines, the land was as much a part of her as she was of it. She knew every inch of it, every secret trail and hidden brook, and in its vast silence, she found her truest self.

Sydney's journey to this point had not been easy. A native of Colorado, she had grown up with a deep love for horses and the wilderness. Her childhood was spent riding through the dense forests and open plains, learning the language of the horses she adored. As she grew older, her passion evolved into a vision: a working farm where she could nurture and care for these majestic creatures.

The path to realizing this dream was fraught with challenges. Sydney faced skeptics who doubted a woman's ability to manage such an endeavor, financial hurdles that seemed insurmountable, and personal trials that tested her resolve. Yet, Sydney persevered with a spirit as untamed as the horses she cared for. She worked multiple jobs, saved every penny, earned a master's degree in equine science, and poured her heart and soul into building her farm from the ground up.

Sydney felt a brimming sense of accomplishment as she looked out over the fields bathed in the golden light of dawn, with the soft nickers of horses breaking the morning stillness. Her farm was not just a business; it was a place where she could share her knowledge and love for horses with others.

The farm was also a refuge for animals in need. Sydney often took in rescue horses, rehabilitating them with patience and gentle guidance. Her approach to horse care was rooted in understanding and respect. She believed in natural horsemanship, a philosophy she had embraced wholeheartedly, advocating for a partnership with the horse rather than dominance over it.

Each horse had a story, and Sydney knew them all - the abandoned, the abused, the misunderstood. She worked tirelessly to heal physical wounds and broken spirits. In their recovery, she often found parallels with her own life, lessons of trust, healing, and transformation.

Sydney's reputation as a skilled horsewoman grew. She started offering training sessions, clinics on natural horsemanship, and even a sanctuary space for those seeking a respite from the world's chaos. Her deep connection with the land and the animals made her an exceptional teacher; her lessons imbued her with an understanding that extended beyond the technical aspects of horse care.

However, the most significant impact of her

farm was on Sydney herself. In the horses, she found a mirror to her soul, reflecting her strength, resilience, and capacity for unconditional love. They had taught her the power of silent communication, the importance of being present, and the beauty of forming connections without words.

Sydney continued her work. Each movement was a silent dance between her and the animals she loved. Her farm was more than just a place; it was a living, breathing entity and a reflection of her spirit and bond with the natural world. Her Australian shepherd, Blue, rested nearby, his ears perking up as a distant sound broke the silence.

A figure emerged from the dense thicket bordering her property. Weary and faltering, it was a man on horseback. They moved with an urgency that spoke of desperation and pain. Honed by years of living in harmony with nature, Sydney's instincts sprang into action. She recognized the horse. A wild Mustang she had previously worked with, relocating it to Colorado. She recalled its resistance to bond with humans, the wild pull of freedom strong in its soul.

As the man and horse crossed the threshold of her land, the man slumped and fell to the ground.

Blue barked a signal of alert as Sydney rushed to the man's side. Her years of experience in outdoor first aid guided her swift response. She assessed his injuries with a practiced eye. Without hesitation, she radioed emergency services, her voice steady as she requested a helicopter evacuation.

Sydney skillfully maneuvered Jason's dislocated leg. Her hands moved with precision and care, echoing her extensive knowledge and unspoken connection to the wilderness and its unpredictability. Jason's eyes momentarily flickered open, meeting Sydney's determined gaze. In that brief exchange, a silent understanding passed between them — a mutual recognition of survival and strength. With her untamed hair and weathered face, Sydney embodied the resilience of the land she called home. Her farm, a sanctuary for wild spirits and broken souls, had become her world, where she healed more than just injured animals.

As she stabilized Jason's chest with bandages, her mind wandered to the countless days she had spent nurturing the wounded creatures on her farm. Each animal, from the smallest injured bird to the most spirited horse, had taught her the value of patience, empathy, and the healing power of a gentle touch. Sydney's life, much like the rugged terrain of Colorado, was filled with challenges and triumphs, all shaping her spirit.

Jason, caught in a haze of pain and confusion, tried to speak but only managed a hoarse whisper. Sydney hushed him gently, her presence calming amidst the chaos. She glanced up as the sound of the approaching helicopter intensified, signaling the arrival of help and the end of Jason's harrowing journey. But for Sydney, this was just another day on her farm, another life touched by her compassion, another story etched into the soul of the wilderness she loved.

The Mustang lingered in the near distance, gaze fixed on Jason. With no more left to give, it melted to the ground in a silent surrender. The scene was a powerful reminder of the untamed beauty and unexpected encounters that defined life in this remote corner of Colorado.

The roar of the helicopter blades churned above, slicing through the tranquility of the Colorado wilderness. For Jason, this sound was a haunting echo of his past, a reminder of a day he had tried to forget but never could. His mind, in a haze of pain and memories, transported him back to the heat and turmoil of his last combat mission.

He was astride a robust, loyal horse, moving stealthily with his fellow Army Rangers through enemy territory. The mission had been clear, but the enemy was not. They were an unseen, unpredictable force, much like the wild Mustang he had come to know in these mountains. The day was progressing with the usual caution, the unit relying on their rigorous training and the instincts of their horses to guide them.

Suddenly, the calm was shattered by the deafening sound of gunfire. Bullets zipped through the air, creating terror and confusion. Jason's horse reared up in panic, its instincts kicking in, trying to escape the chaos. Jason gripped the reins tightly, attempting to calm the animal. Fear hung thick in the air, the danger all too real.

As Jason's steed reared for freedom, a mortar round struck, violently thrusting man and horse backward. Jason pirouetted in the air, catching two rounds before he hit the ground. His horse landed lifeless beside him, offering him cover and concealment from the flying hot lead.

In the ensuing battle, the Rangers fought

valiantly. Two horses, startled by the sudden erup-
tion of violence, threw their riders to the ground.
One of his comrades, a young soldier with a bright
future, was instantly struck down by enemy fire, his
life slipping away amidst the dust and the blood.

As the fight raged, a Blackhawk helicopter sig-
naled a chance of survival. As it quickly entered the
scene, it unleashed a deadly firestorm from above,
neutralizing the enemy. The Blackhawk circled in
a patrolling pattern, ensuring it was safe for the
rescue chopper to land. One of the rescue medics
reached Jason's side. "I got you," the medic's voice
projected over the roar of rotor blades.

Amidst the relief of rescue, a heart-wrenching
sight caught Jason's eye—his horse lay lifeless on
the ground, an innocent victim caught in the cross-
fire of human conflict. The image was devastat-
ing—a reminder of the senselessness of war. This
noble creature, once full of life and spirit, now lay
still, its eyes closed forever to the world it once
roamed freely. And if the scene wasn't poignant
enough, Jason's eyes caught two medics carrying
his fallen friend to the chopper.

A surge of sorrow enveloped Jason. His gaze
shifted from the fallen horse to his fallen comrade

and back again. It was a moment that etched itself into his memory, a painful reminder of the cost of war, not just in human lives but in the lives of all creatures caught in its wake.

In his delirious state, Jason's mind oscillated between past and present. The sound of the rescue helicopter landing on Sydney's farm blurred with the echoes of that fateful day. His gaze shifted to the Mustang, now lying in the field, stirring a poignant mix of grief and confusion.

As the emergency team loaded Jason into the helicopter, tears rolled down his cheek, his eyes affixed on this equine savior. As the chopper lifted off, Sydney's attention turned to the Mustang. Her expertise in equestrian care and the teachings she had imbibed since childhood made her the perfect guardian for the horse in Jason's absence.

The helicopter's departure left Sydney in a thoughtful solitude. She reflected on her journey—a life dedicated to the wilderness, horses, and the healing they offered. Unlike Jason, who had found his connection with horses later in life, Sydney had embraced this bond from her earliest memories. It was a bond that now extended to the Mustang, whose fate remained uncertain.

Jason awoke in the hospital, disoriented but alive. The sterile white of the room clashed with the vivid, chaotic memories that still gripped his mind. He could still feel the Mustang's powerful gait beneath him, a rhythm that had become a lifeline in the wilderness of his tormented soul. Lying there, his body ached from the physical ordeal, but it was the wounds within that throbbed the most.

As consciousness filtered through the haze of painkillers, his first thoughts were of the Mustang. That horse had become more than a companion; it had become a reflection of his struggles, a symbol of the raw and rugged path to healing he had embarked. The horse's fierce independence and resilience in the face of adversity mirrored Jason's journey through the labyrinth of PTSD and the ghosts of moral injury that haunted him.

The sound of the door opening drew his attention. His parents stepped into the room. Their faces, fraught with worry and relief, brought a sense of grounding to his turbulent emotions. As they approached, their expressions softened, transforming into smiles that carried a warmth he had almost forgotten. Their presence was a balm to his restless spirit, a reminder of a life beyond the battlefield and the wilderness.

His mother's gentle touch, brushing the hair from his forehead, reminded him of simpler times, childhood laughter and carefree days. His father stood awkwardly to the side, his eyes conveying a depth of concern that words could never fully express. Jason burst out with a tearful, crying laugh as his mother embraced her only son.

They spoke of mundane things at first, carefully skirting around the shadows that lingered in the corners of the room. But as the minutes stretched into hours, the conversation shifted, delving into the deeper currents of Jason's life. He found himself opening up about the nightmares that stalked him, the memories of his last mission that played on an endless loop in his mind. His parents listened, their faces masked with empathy and pain as he recounted the events that had led him to this point.

It was his father who first broached the subject of the Mustang. "That horse," he said, his voice tinged with awe and understanding, "it's more than just an animal to you, isn't it?" Jason nodded, feeling a surge of emotion at the mention of the

Mustang. He spoke of their first encounter, how the wild creature had mirrored his sense of being lost and untethered. He shared the moments of connection, mutual understanding, and their unspoken bond.

As he spoke, his parents saw the transformation that had begun in their son. They recognized the parallels between Jason's journey and the teachings of natural horsemanship, a philosophy his father had embraced and shared since childhood. "Remember what I used to tell you," His father said softly, "about the way of the horse. It's about mutual respect, not domination? Every interaction a dialogue, not a demand?"

Those words, imbued with the wisdom of natural horsemanship, resonated with Jason now more than ever. They were not just lessons in horse training; they were life lessons. The Mustang had become a living embodiment of those teachings, guiding him back to a place of balance and harmony.

Jason's mother, her eyes glistening with unshed tears, spoke of the healing power of connection. "You've always bonded with horses, even when you were little. They could sense your heart, your true intentions," she said. "Maybe this Mustang is your way of finding peace, of coming back to yourself."

The conversation flowed into the evening, unveiling shared memories, hopes, and fears. Jason talked about his plans for the Mustang and wanted to provide a sanctuary where they could heal and grow. His parents listened, their support unwavering, their belief in him a steady flame in the darkness of his doubts.

As night fell and the hospital room grew quiet, Jason lay back on his pillow, his mind swirling with thoughts. The path ahead would not be easy, but he no longer felt alone. In the bond with the Mustang, in the love of his family, he had found a source of strength that would guide him through the journey ahead.

The transformative path lay open before him, intertwined with the fate of the Mustang he had grown to cherish. Together, they would navigate the rugged terrain of healing and recovery.

CHAPTER 14

Reunion and Recovery

In the quiet of the hospital room, Jason lay contemplating the ceiling, his thoughts as fragmented as the patterns on the tiles. His body was a map of bruises and bandages, but it was his mind that felt the most battered. The echoes of his past life. A life spent more in survival than living—mingled with the reality of the present. The world continued its rhythm outside, oblivious to the turmoil within these walls. Birds chirped, heralding the break of dawn, but for Jason, time seemed suspended, anchored in a sea of introspection.

Sydney's visits to the hospital were like a gentle breeze, refreshing and vitalizing. Each time she walked into the room, there was an unspoken shift in the atmosphere, as if the walls themselves breathed easier. Her calm demeanor was a soothing contrast to the clinical, impersonal surroundings of the hospital.

With every visit, Sydney brought with her an aura of tranquility. Her understanding eyes, always so full of empathy, seemed to see beyond the physical injuries, acknowledging the deeper, unseen wounds Jason grappled with. Her presence was a tangible reminder of the world outside these walls. A world of open skies and endless possibilities.

As she settled beside Jason's bed, there was a comfortable ease in her manner, a naturalness that made the small hospital room feel less confined. Her gentle smile, unforced and genuine, was a beacon of warmth. It wasn't just her words that conveyed care; it was her entire being, radiating kindness and compassion.

The conversations between Sydney and Jason flowed effortlessly, punctuated by moments of shared laughter and reflective silences. With each visit, they peeled back layers of their lives, revealing the vulnerabilities and strengths that defined them. Sydney spoke of her life on the farm, of the challenges and joys of working with animals, her words painting vivid images in Jason's mind, transporting him beyond the hospital room.

Jason found himself opening up with each of Sydney's visits. He shared anecdotes from his past, spoke of his fears and hopes, and even ventured into the guarded territories of his dreams and aspirations. It was a revelation, this ease of sharing, this feeling of being understood without the need for elaborate explanations.

There was a subtle yet undeniable chemistry building between them. It was in the way their eyes met and lingered, in the comfortable silences that spoke volumes, in the laughter that came a little too easily. With every story shared, every memory recounted, they were solidifying a connection, each moment pulling them closer and deepening their mutual understanding and affection.

The spark of a developing relationship was there, kindling slowly, its glow evident in their every interaction. It wasn't a blazing fire but rather a gentle flame, warming them with the promise of something deeper, something more. In Sydney's attentive listening and thoughtful responses, Jason felt connected to someone who cared for his well-being and resonated with his soul.

As Sydney updated Jason on the Mustang's progress, their conversations often veered into personal territories, exploring the emotions and experiences that paralleled their lives with the horse's journey. Discussing the challenges of healing and the beauty of resilience, the foundations of a budding relationship were laid—one built on mutual respect, shared experiences, and a deep, intuitive understanding of each other's worlds.

The Mustang's path to recovery was a slow and deliberate process that Sydney navigated with a blend of expertise and intuition. As she entered the paddock, her presence brought a calm assurance. Her movements around the Mustang were measured and respectful, acknowledging the horse's space and mind. She understood that healing, for creatures as intuitive as horses, was as much emotional and psychological as it was physical.

As Sydney worked with the Mustang, her actions blended professional skills and deep empathy. She would often speak to the horse softly, reassuringly, offering encouragement as she gently tended to its needs. While managing the horse's injuries, her hands were healing physical wounds and communicating trust and safety. The Mustang's response was overall positive. Once wary and distant, its eyes held a softer, more curious gaze.

With each passing day, the Mustang's recovery mirrored the gradual change in its demeanor. From the stiff, guarded posture it initially held, it began to move fluidly, its muscles relaxing, its steps more confident yet calm. Sydney celebrated these small milestones, knowing each represented a significant leap in the Mustang's journey back to wholeness.

Sydney's character shone through in these interactions. Her patience was more than a professional requirement. It was her nature. She approached the Mustang as a partner on its road to recovery. Her understanding of the Mustang's trauma went beyond textbook knowledge; it was rooted in a deep, intuitive connection with the animal.

Her approach to healing was holistic. Sydney understood that the Mustang's recovery was more than healing its physical injuries. She would help restore its spirit and its trust in the world. She spent hours with the Mustang, not just in active care but often just being present, allowing the horse to get accustomed to her presence and to understand that she was a friend, not a foe.

This patience and empathy were reflective of Sydney's journey. She had built her life around understanding and helping animals, recognizing in them the same complexities of emotion and trauma that humans experience. Her farm was not just a place for physical rehabilitation but a sanctuary for emotional healing for animals and people like Jason.

As Sydney shared these experiences with Jason, the Mustang's progress symbolized hope and resilience. She drew parallels between the Mustang's healing and Jason's, highlighting the importance of patience, trust, and the understanding that recovery is a journey, not a destination. In these stories, Jason saw the Mustang's journey, Sydney's dedication and compassion, her unwavering belief in the power of healing, and the strength of the spirit, whether equine or human.

Sydney and the Mustang's bond beautifully intertwined trust and understanding. It was a relationship built on mutual respect and a shared journey of overcoming adversity. In her interactions with the Mustang, Sydney exemplified a person

who healed with her hands and heart, embody-
ing the essence of resilience and hope. But Sydney could feel something was missing. Although
connected, the Mustang's eyes were often distant,
searching.

Back in the hospital, as Jason's physical wounds
began to mend, the landscape of his inner world
was transforming. The therapy sessions, though
grueling, were carving pathways through the once
impenetrable forest of his memories and emotions.
Each session, with its revelations and realizations,
was like a ray of light piercing through the canopy,
illuminating the shadows of his past. The presence
of his psychologist, who was also a combat veteran,
added a layer of depth and understanding to these
sessions. This shared experience created a bridge
of trust and empathy, allowing Jason to traverse
the rugged terrain of his memories with someone
who truly understood the language of war and its
aftermath.

As these sessions progressed, Jason began to
realize talk therapy's immense importance and effi-
cacy. It was more than recounting events or express-
ing feelings; it was unraveling the complex tapestry
of his experiences, thoughts, and emotions. The

psychologist's approach, which combined professional expertise with personal insight, helped Jason to see the value in verbalizing his struggles. He learned that speaking about his experiences, particularly with someone who had walked a similar path, was not a sign of weakness but a courageous step toward healing. Articulating his memories and emotions was cathartic, helping him to release the burdens he had carried for so long. This newfound appreciation for talk therapy marked a significant milestone in his recovery, opening doors to deeper understanding and lasting wholeness.

Amidst this journey of self-discovery and healing, the visits from friends and family served as a vital source of support and comfort, anchoring him to a world beyond the hospital's walls. His mother's visits, particularly, comforted his weary soul. Each time she entered the room, her presence was like a warm embrace, enveloping him in a sense of unconditional love and understanding that only a mother could provide. She would sit by his bed, her hand in his, a physical connection that grounded him. Her gentle and soothing voice would recount tales of his childhood, reminiscing days filled with laughter, play, and the carefree innocence of youth. These stories, woven with love and nostalgia, transported Jason back to a simpler time, creating a bridge between his past and present.

In her presence, Jason rediscovered parts of himself that he had long forgotten. Her memories of him as a child, curious, spirited, and full of life, contrasted with the hardened soldier he had become. They resonated with a truth that he could not deny. Her anecdotes, often laced with humor and affection, reminded him of the values and dreams he once held. As she spoke, it wasn't just the stories that captivated him but the unspoken reminders of her enduring love and belief in him despite the paths he had walked and the scars he had gathered. Through her eyes, he saw not just the soldier tormented by war but the son she had always cherished and the man he had the potential to become. Her visits were more than just a mother's care; they were a gentle nudge toward self-compassion and a reminder of the enduring power of familial love.

His sister's visits to the hospital were like a burst of sunshine on a cloudy day, infusing the room with laughter and lightness. She had a way of teasing him that was both affectionate and irreverent, a playful banter that seemed to dance around the room, dispelling the somberness that often lingered in the air. Her jokes, quick-witted and full of life, frequently caught Jason off guard, sparking laughter that felt both surprising and deeply healing. It was a laughter that bubbled up from within, a reminder of lighter times, unburdened by the weight of his recent experiences.

Her presence had a transformative effect on the atmosphere. The hospital's clinical environment seemed to soften and brighten with her arrival. She brought with her stories from the outside world, anecdotes about friends and family, and tales of everyday adventures. These stories were windows to a world that Jason had been temporarily cut off from, a world that continued to spin with energy and color. She painted a picture of life's vibrancy through lively narratives and playful teasing. A renewed life that awaited him beyond the hospital's confines.

With his sister, Jason found himself slipping effortlessly back into the role of a brother. Their interactions were a dance of mutual affection. They shared history, a dynamic that had been a part of their relationship since childhood. She reminded him of the many roles he played in life—not just as a soldier or a patient, but as a brother, a friend, a mentor. Her visits helped him reconnect with aspects of his identity that had been overshadowed by his military service and subsequent recovery. In her company, Jason felt a sense of normalcy, a touchstone to the person he was before the war and the person he could be again. Her presence was a vivid reminder that, despite his challenges, the essence of his identity remained intact, waiting to be rediscovered and embraced.

Visits from his military buddies were particularly poignant. They didn't need many words to communicate; their shared experiences in the service had forged a bond beyond language. Jason found a sense of camaraderie and belonging in their silent understanding and respectful nods. They spoke of their struggles and triumphs, offering perspectives that resonated with Jason's journey. Their presence was a reminder that he wasn't alone in his battle, that the brotherhood they formed in the service extended beyond the battlefield.

With each visit, Jason's dialogue with his visitors subtly shifted. He began to speak more openly about his experiences, not just as a soldier but as a man who had seen the depths of human suffering and resilience. He talked about his therapy sessions, the insights he was gaining, and his emerging understanding of his PTSD and moral injury.

It was a sign that he was beginning to reconcile the incongruent parts of his identity—the soldier, the survivor, the wounded warrior. He was learning to accept his past, not as a burden but as a series of chapters in the larger story of his life. His narrative was changing from one of conflict and pain to one of understanding and growth.

In these exchanges, there was a noticeable change in how Jason interacted with his visitors. He listened intently, empathized deeply, and shared more of himself. His responses reflected his experiences and his growing ability to see the world through others' eyes. This shift in dialogue indicated a significant step in his healing journey. He was recovering from his wounds; moreover, he was transcending them.

As Jason's physical strength returned, so did his emotional and psychological fortitude. The support of his friends and family, coupled with his therapy, was helping him leave behind the shadows of his past. He was beginning to embrace all aspects of who he was—the pain, the joy, the strength, and the vulnerability. This holistic acceptance was the true hallmark of his healing, a journey not just back to himself but toward a new, integrated identity forged through the fire of experience and tempered with the wisdom of introspection.

As the days passed, the connection between Jason and Sydney blossomed into something rich and profound. Sydney's visits, marked by thoughtful conversations and shared experiences, became the highlights of Jason's days in the hospital. The photographs she brought of the Mustang were visual representations of transformation and hope. Jason saw a journey of change in those pictures that paralleled his own—from defensiveness and isolation to trust and connection. The Mustang, once wild and unapproachable, now calm and grounded, served as a powerful metaphor for his healing process.

These moments of clarity, as he looked at the photographs, deepened Jason's understanding of healing. It wasn't a solitary path but an interconnected journey where the healing of one soul could inspire and aid in the healing of another. Jason saw his journey in the Mustang's eyes—a reflection of his challenges and strides. And in Sydney's company, he found a caregiver, a friend, and a kindred spirit—someone who understood the silent language of healing and the power of connection.

Their conversation naturally flowed into possibilities and dreams as they sat together, flipping through the photographs. Inspired by their shared experiences and the lessons learned along the way, they began to envision a program for veterans at Sydney's farm in the mountains. This program would be a sanctuary, much like the farm had been for the Mustang, offering equine-assisted learning and therapy.

The idea was to create a space where veterans could find healing through the power of connection with horses. They discussed integrating the lessons Jason had learned through his recovery—the importance of trust, the power of vulnerability, and the strength found in facing one's fears. Sydney shared her insights on equine therapy, explaining how working with horses could help veterans rebuild confidence, establish connections, and learn to communicate non-verbally, tapping into emotions and often hard-to-articulate experiences.

They planned to create a holistic program that combined the therapeutic benefits of horse interactions with counseling and group support sessions. They envisioned a place where veterans could come to heal and find a sense of purpose and community. This farm, nestled in the tranquility of the mountains, would be a haven for those seeking to reconcile their war experiences and integrate the different parts of their identities.

As they spoke, their excitement and passion for the project were evident. This plan was a culmination of their shared journey. It was a way to give back and help others walking the challenging path they knew all too well. In this shared vision, Jason and Sydney saw a future for themselves and a beacon of hope for others. Jason and Sydney were poised at the brink of a new endeavor that promised healing, growth, and new beginnings for many.

CHAPTER 15

Inner Summits

The rising sun cast burning yellow-red hues over the landscape. It had been a year since Jason had left the confines of the hospital, and the world seemed to hold a new promise. He and Sydney had been tirelessly working on their equine veteran program, a dream slowly manifesting. Their relationship, a once fragile bud, had blossomed into a deep, committed partnership. For Jason, this was more than a romance; it was a journey into what a healthy, mature relationship could be.

At the heart of their program was Eclipse—the Mustang Jason had grown profoundly attached. Naming the horse *Eclipse* was symbolic.

It represented a rare and significant event that brought about change. This name reflected the transformative impact of the Mustang. Just as an eclipse marks a moment of awe and transition, the horse signified a turning point in Jason's life.

Under Jason's care, Eclipse had transformed from a once wild and unapproachable creature into a responsive and trusting partner. Together, they practiced natural horsemanship, a dance of subtle cues and mutual respect. Whether on the ground or mounted, their synergy was evident – a testament to the healing power of connection.

The program, conceived from the shared vision of Jason and Sydney, began to flourish, transforming into a sanctuary of healing and hope for veterans. With the support of a funding grant from the Veterans Administration, their dream was bolstered by tangible resources, allowing them to lay a strong foundation for their initiative. Their commitment and dedication also led to the establishment of a nonprofit organization, further solidifying their mission to aid fellow veterans. This strategic move opened doors to attract prominent benefactors whose generosity and belief in the cause ensured the program's sustainability and growth.

As the program commenced, it started on a modest scale, focusing on quality and personalization. Ensuring each participant received the attention and care they needed was paramount. They began by accepting small groups of veterans referred by regional VA centers. This approach allowed Jason and Sydney to create a more intimate and impactful experience, catering to the unique needs of each individual.

In these early stages, Jason found himself deeply connected to the veterans who came to the farm. He saw reflections of his journey in theirs – the initial reluctance to open up, the unfamiliarity with the horses, and the cautious steps toward healing. As they interacted with the horses, especially with Eclipse, Jason observed their gradual but significant changes. The veterans learned to communicate with the animals, finding peace and understanding that often eluded them in other aspects of their lives.

The bond between the veterans and the horses became a powerful catalyst for change. Through grooming, riding, and caring for the horses, the veterans developed new skills and rediscovered parts of themselves lost or suppressed due to their military experiences. With their intuitive nature, the horses provided a non-judgmental space for the veterans to express themselves, facilitating a form of healing that words alone could not achieve.

The program's growth was steady and meaningful. Each session and interaction added to the healing and recovery of the veterans. It also had a positive impact on Jason and Sydney. They created a community where understanding, empathy, and mutual support were the cornerstones.

As word of the program's success spread, the interest and support from the community grew. Having experienced significant strides in their healing journey, the initial group of veterans became advocates for the program, sharing their stories and encouraging fellow veterans to participate.

One morning, Jason invited Sydney for a ride. His eyes had a certain intensity, a mix of determination and vulnerability. They rode in comfortable silence, the rhythmic sound of the horses' hooves a soothing melody. Unbeknownst to Sydney, their destination was the cliff where Jason's life had nearly ended.

As they approached the cliff, memories flooded back, each a reminder of the day that had changed everything. Sydney, recognizing the place, felt a surge of apprehension. "Jason, you don't have to prove anything," she said softly, her voice laced with concern.

Jason and Eclipse stood by the cliff, their silhouette etched against the expanse of rock. He dismounted with a grace that spoke of his newfound physical and emotional balance. Once clouded with turmoil, his gaze now held a clarity from deep introspection. "I'm not here to relive the past, Syd," he said, his voice resonating with a steadiness that mirrored his inner calm. "I'm here to close a chapter." Turning to face Sydney, his eyes reflected a serenity born from conquering inner tumult. "This place. It represents where I once faced my biggest fears. Yet, I've realized the most daunting mountain was never this cliff. It was the 'Intermountain' – the arduous, introspective journey within."

Leaning against the cliff, Jason spread his arms wide, embracing the rock around him. He closed his eyes, inhaled deeply, and seemed to absorb the essence of the mountain and the world around him. When he spoke again, his words flowed with a philosophical depth. "Each step of the journey, every hurdle I encountered, has been a lesson in self-discovery. It wasn't just about scaling physical heights or battling visible enemies. It was about scaling the walls I built around my heart, breathing through the steep ascents of my inner struggles, and reaching the peak of my consciousness."

Sydney absorbed every word as she witnessed Jason's visible transformation. His journey had become a philosophical exploration, a deep dive into the essence of his being. "Conquering," Jason continued, his eyes now open, gazing into the distance, "used to mean overcoming external challenges, proving my strength to the world. But true conquest is internal. It's about finding peace within, understanding the depths of one's soul, and emerging victorious in the battles we fight within our minds and hearts."

His words painted a picture of rebirth and enlightenment. "The real battle," Jason mused, "is waged against the shadows and doubts within, not in the outer world. Our greatest victories are when we conquer our fears, insecurities, and traumas and find that serenity that resonates from within."

As he stood there, a figure of resilience and wisdom, Jason embodied the essence of a journey that many seek but few complete — the journey

of knowing thy self, facing one's cliffs, and finding tranquility beyond the arduous climbs of life.
This moment by the cliff did not end a chapter in
Jason's life. It was the beginning of a new narrative
– one where every challenge was an opportunity
for growth, and every summit reached echoed the
power of the human spirit.

Jason's hand delved into his pocket, retrieving a
cigar, a token of victory and remembrance. In the
Rangers, these rolled leaves had marked the end of
each triumphant mission, a ritual honoring both
success and sacrifice. With reverent precision, he lit
the cigar, its ember glowing like a beacon in the
fading light. As the first wisps of smoke curled into
the air, Jason's voice carried a solemn weight:

"To those wrestling with their shadows, may
they discover the light within and forge a path to
redemption and serenity."

The words hung in the air, a blessing and a
prayer intertwined. Jason inhaled deeply, the familiar taste awakening memories of brotherhood and
loss. As he exhaled, the smoke danced away on the
mountain breeze, carrying with it unspoken stories
of trials overcome and comrades forever absent.

His gaze shifted to Sydney, eyes reflecting a mix

of nostalgia and newfound purpose. "It's time," he said softly, "to return home." The simple phrase held layers of meaning - a journey completed, a chapter closed, and the promise of new beginnings on the horizon.

Jason and Sydney rode side by side, enveloped in contemplative silence, their minds weaving through the lessons learned and the possibilities that lay before them. As they breached the natural boundary of Sydney's farm, a sense of tranquility wrapped them. Jason reached out and held Sydney's hand, their fingers intertwining as they looked across the fields. There, under the expansive Colorado sky, bathed in the warm, golden hues of the setting sun, they observed the veterans interacting with the horses. It was a scene of healing and connection, reflecting the journey they had embarked upon together. In that quiet, serene moment, watching the bonds between the veterans and their equine companions flourish, Jason felt a deep sense of fulfillment and hope, sentiments mirrored in Sydney's gentle grip.

The End.

Where whispers weave through trees,
Two souls adrift, caught in despair's cold breeze.
One, cloaked in silence, burdened by his past,
The other, wild-eyed, with shadows cast.

Both broken, yet beneath the sun's morning glow,
A silent understanding begins to grow.
Man meets horse, in the day's embrace,
Finding solace in the other's face.

Trust, a fragile seed, in darkness sown,
In the quiet wild, where true selves are shown.
From tentative steps, a bond takes flight,
In the vast expanse of the starry night.

Healing whispers in the rustling leaves,
In shared breaths, the heavy heart believes.
With each stride, side by side, they find,
A balm for the body, peace for the mind.

In the bond, a transformation deep,
What was sown in trust, they now reap.
From despair's edge, to the light of dawn,
Together, they emerge, reborn and drawn.

In the wilderness, where their journey began,
Man and horse, united, stand.
A testament to the power, strong and real,
Of a bond that heals, of a love that heals.

www.ingramcontent.com/pod-product-compliance
Lightning Source LLC
Chambersburg PA
CBHW061533310726
48972CB00008B/2435